THE ABORTION OF PACIFIC FLIGHT 571

JOHN HYLTON

FLIGHTSONGBOOKS@GMAIL.COM

Chapter 1   Anchorage Intl Airport

It looked like an invasion.

Against the backdrop of a crystal blue sky, punctuated by white Pillsbury Dough Boy looking clouds, the hundreds of military personnel could be seen running with their M16 rifles held tightly to their sides. Their drab olive fatigues contrasted with the beige, block constructed airport buildings as they raced past. They had arrived at Anchorage International Airport in mass and in great haste. The vehicles, seldom used troop carriers that shined as if waxed daily, had been driven to their destination much faster than for what they were originally designed. Two of them had actually broken down along the highway that leads from Elmendorf Air Force Base, through the city of Anchorage, and onto the airport's access roads, all of which marked with deep jagged pot holes left from the past winter's snows that covered them for over six months.

Thirty-two Airmen, sixteen from each of the two broken down vehicles stood in loose formation along the highway while their comrades continued past in their properly operating and full troop carriers. A quick thinking sergeant flagged down an empty yellow school bus and demanded the alarmed driver, a graying woman in her mid-fifties, to drive them to the airport. No explanations were given. She was left to her own imagination as to the reason for this bizarre event, which left her convinced that terrorists were attacking United States as they had before with the hijacking of airliners and crashing them into the World Trading Center and Pentagon.

At the airport they exited the bus in such haphazard haste that the grey barrels of the rifles were clacking against each other with a sound not unlike the igniting of a string of firecrackers on the Fourth of July. The men quickly joined the others as their officers directed them into their tactical positions, ready for the arrival of some threat, some dangerous event, of which they had no idea. In fact, only the Commander and four of his subordinates knew what was really going on. They were waiting for the arrival of a civilian airliner, a Boeing 737, Pacific Airlines Flight 571.

Most of the airmen had not even fired an M16 since Basic Training at Lackland Air Force Base, Texas, which for some were two to four years earlier. They had been rushed out of their barracks and classrooms, distributed rifles, and loaded into troop carriers for the harried thirty-minute ride from Elmendorf Air Force Base to Anchorage International Airport. They were told not to ask questions, to do what they were directed, and to be ready for armed conflict. Many of their stomachs were churned up in the nervousness that comes from fear, heightened by the complete lack of information about the situation, and absolutely no experience in armed military exercises.

The briefings had been short but effective, directing hundreds of armed airmen to their assigned positions. It was imperative that all available airmen were in position before the arrival of the aircraft that would arrive within the hour. Airport access roads were blocked. Personnel were stationed outside and inside the terminal.

Hallways and ticket counter areas were secured. All airport employees, uniformed airline ticket agents, baggage checkers, security agents, flight attendants, and pilots were ordered outside and away from the terminal. They were taken to a secure area, a rent-a-car return lot that was now surrounded by armed military personnel. They were joined by members of the public that had been waiting for arriving passengers. Attempts to get answers from their guards were fruitless. Their unanswered questions steadily gave rise to panic, which began to spread throughout the secured parking lot like an out of control fire blazing though dry grass. No one would, or could, explain to them what was going on. There wasn't time for that luxury.

The guards knew nothing of the reason for all of this, just that they had orders to keep everyone in the lot. It was chaotic order, organized pandemonium. Once secure, there was no movement inside the terminal, as if it had become a ghost town.

The weather was perfect for a military operation. Unlimited visibility, the temperature was 62 degrees Fahrenheit, unseasonably warm for a March afternoon. The Airmen were dressed in fatigues with no necessity of coats that could impede the agility required to deal with the upcoming tactic. They were more mobile this way.

High above the airport's runways and ramps stood the stately new control tower. Rising two hundred feet in the air with a glass cab on top, it had now become the best vantage point to witness the military take-over going on below. In the top floor of the tower were four men, all FAA Air Traffic Controllers assigned to various responsibilities, including ground control, clearance delivery, and take-off and landing authorizations. On the floor below, without windows, controllers sat at their radar screens providing directions to arriving and departing aircraft. They were totally unaware of what was happening beneath them. It was quiet in the radar room. This happened to be one of the quietest times in recent history, due to the fact that no aircraft were arriving from the southeast due to San Francisco's fogged in condition. Only one plane had been able to depart San Francisco. The radar controllers' screens worked an area within a forty mile radius of Anchorage and were expecting Pacific Flight 571 to check in with them any minute.

One floor above the control tower personnel continued to watch the unusual happenings two hundred feet below. They watched as a group of twenty airmen raced to the bottom of the tower. A buzzer rang just beside the chair of the tower supervisor, signaling him that someone was seeking entry through the locked and secure door at the ground level.

"This is the control tower."

"This is Lieutenant Thomas of the US Air Force. We have orders to secure the tower. Open the door!"

"Okay," replied the tower supervisor, as he pushed another button to unlock the lower door, "but, we'd sure like to know what's going on!"

Within sixty seconds the first elevator full of the military airmen arrived at the cab level. Within another sixty seconds they had completely commandeered both top floors of the control tower and had placed Air Force operators at all positions. The civilian controllers were taken down the elevators and into awaiting vans. They were driven to the secure parking lot. No explanations were given.

The United States Air Force now had complete control of every facet of Anchorage International Airport in anticipation of the arrival of Pacific Flight 571. And it had taken less than twenty minutes.

Nervousness over the assignment had long since given way to the pure excitement brought on by the feverish haste of the maneuver. Some had initially thought it was a drill but soon determined this was the real thing, a military operation that most likely would involve hostile fire. It had to be terrorists. Only one person knew the real story and the politics behind this affair. The potential impact upon his ambitious career this opportunity presented was significant.

Major General Keith Dryer was in full dress uniform with two brightly shining stars on each shoulder and six square inches of multi-colored ribbons adorning his chest. He stood proudly at his makeshift command center on the roof of the passenger terminal. Here, he had a clear view of all the events and could easily watch the arrival of Pacific Flight 571. The roof was flat and had a four-foot high ledge boundary behind which he could duck for cover should gunfire erupt. A patio set had been brought in complete with umbrella and table at which he could sit and drink his Starbucks latte as he cockily watched hundreds of men do his bidding.

Earlier, General Dryer had cleverly briefed his few subordinates only what they needed to know. What they did not need to know was the political undertone for this entire maneuver. He counted on the probability that all would assume that an extremely dangerous and armed terrorist was aboard Pacific Flight 571.

General Dryer was an expert at making sure adrenalin pumped to high levels. How else could this highly motivated Flag Officer impress the President? After all, this is the President's call. Even as he was engaged in the somewhat misleading briefing to his commanders, visions of becoming Chairman of the Joint Chiefs of Staff paraded in his mind.

It had happened never before, that such an armada of armed personnel had been formed to meet an arriving civilian jetliner. They had taken up tactical positions around Pacific Airlines Flight 571 as it finally pulled into Gate B2.

Twenty armed personnel crouched in the gate area with weapons ready. It could not be known for sure whether the subject would exit the aircraft via the outside stairs to the ramp or directly through the jetway into the gate area.

Whichever egress he chose he could not get away. He would most likely meet horrible consequences if he attempted to escape capture or resist arrest. All contingencies were covered. The man was aboard Pacific Flight 571 from San Francisco.

All assumed the man they were waiting for was a passenger, some terrorist that had threatened to detonate a bomb or ram the airplane into a building. They had been briefed that the perpetrator was posing as an airline captain and was uniformed as such.

It might have gone off without a hitch, if only one young and inexperienced Airman hadn't put so much nervous pressure on the trigger. It hadn't been a conscious shoot. It was just and unexplained tensing of a muscle that had dreadful consequences.

General Dryer had prepared for this possible outcome. He had seen to it that there would be no intervention by local law enforcement. His orders were to keep this a total military operation. Secrecy of the details was mandatory, especially for future cover-ups of the event should the press start prying into the event. The President of the United States himself had made that perfectly clear.

Chapter 2   San Francisco

Pacific Airline President Sam Pickering lived in a beautiful large waterfront home along the shores of the San Francisco Bay. However, even at seven thousand square feet, and at a value of approximately two million dollars, the Pickering home was considered average by comparison to many of the huge estates along the bay.

He had been President of Pacific Airlines for four years. The Airline had operated in the west since its inception in 1959. In 23 years they had grown from two propeller-driven aircraft to a fleet of over 60 Boeing 737s.

He had just finished breakfast when the important call came in from the head of the Federal Aviation Administration, Noel Howard. They had been casual friends for years and Pacific benefited from the relationship of its President to the Administrator of the F.A.A.

"Sam, I have urgent business with you."

Sam's first thought was, "Oh no, there's been an accident."

"What is it, Noel?"

"You've got a cancelled flight to Anchorage today."

"Yes, that's correct."

"You've also got that specially equipped aircraft with "HUD II."

"But…" Sam attempted to enter in this one-sided conversation.

"Never mind the 'buts,' this is all worked out and comes from orders by the President himself."

Noel took another five minutes and explained the rest of the story.

Sam Pickering did not object. After hanging up with Noel Howard, he immediately dialed Pacific Airlines Chief Pilot, Rusty Ward.

"Rusty, who do we have that is checked out in HUD II?"

"Only Ross Powers," replied Ward, "…he's the expert."

"Fine, give me his phone number. I'll tell you later what's going on."

Ross Powers had been a pilot with Pacific Airlines since its inception.. He had flown every type of aircraft the company owned and was now enjoying flying as captain on the new Boeing 737-800, the most recent addition to Pacific's fleet.

He was the only pilot yet trained on the latest technology, HUD II, a heads up guidance system that would soon allow an aircraft to take off in zero visibility.

The current technology, HUD I, required a minimum runway visual range (RVR) reading of 300 feet for takeoff.

Even though Ross was trained and certified to fly HUD II, the aircraft installation of the instrument was still in the testing phase, and the F.A.A. had not yet authorized its procedure for use in passenger carrying operations.

Ross had been scheduled today to test fly the one 737-800 that was equipped with the experimental HUD II. However, the fog bank that had been lying over the entire San Francisco area since late the night before caused the cancellation of all flights, including test flights. The zero visibility conditions at the airport made it even dangerous to taxi an aircraft, let alone takeoff. There were certainly no arrivals occurring. There were no flights of any kind, commercial, private, or flight test, departing or arriving San Francisco today.

Technology was moving at a rapid pace to develop methods by which commercial airplanes could operate in low visibility conditions. The nation's economy was affected by cancelled and delayed flights, not to mention the profits of the airlines themselves.

Over the years equipment and procedures were developed allowing aircraft to land and takeoff in lower and lower visibility conditions. For landing, "Category I" had been the earliest technology for precision approaches, those providing vertical descent guidance with a glide slope indicator as well as horizontal guidance by way of a "localizer" frequency receiver, which detected signals from a facility located near the runway.

"Category I" permitted aircraft to descend along the glide slope to a point 200 feet above the field elevation before going "missed" if the runway environment was not seen by the pilots by that point. "Category II" technology lowered that "Decision Height" to 100 feet. "Category III," the latest technology allowed the approach to continue to just 50 feet above the field before pilots were required to have established visual contact with the runway.

If the pilots could not see the approach or runway lights by that point a "missed approach" would be commenced. At 50 feet it would not be unusual for the landing gear to actually touch the runway during the go-around. It didn't matter, the landing was still aborted and the pilots would "take it around."

Engineers continued to work on "Category IV" technology that would someday allow landings in zero visibility conditions

Take-offs, however, required less visibility than landings. Normally, only 600 feet of "Runway Visual Range" (RVR) was required for most aircraft to take off. However, another relatively new technology, "Heads Up

Display" (HUD) allowed so equipped aircraft to take off with forward visibility of just 300 feet.

The HUD device was a pull down, see through screen with which the pilot could more easily maintain directional guidance down the runway during take-off. Once off the ground and in flight, visibility could go to zero and the aircraft could continue with complete reliance on instruments for navigation. "HUD II" would eventually allow zero visibility takeoffs.

Ross Powers and his family resided within fifteen minutes of the San Francisco terminal. This was unlike most airline pilot families who, because of only having to originate trips three or four times a month, would normally choose to live far from the airport. Many commuted to their base from other states.

Ross felt that the only negative factor to this profession he otherwise dearly loved and enjoyed was the time it required him to be away from his family on multi-day trips. He never really enjoyed layovers at various cities on Pacific's routes even though the hotel accommodations were excellent.

He missed Mary and their four children whenever he was away and would often take a family member on a two or three day flight. The decision to live close to the airport was borne out of a desire to be absent from his family as little as possible. Mary would drive Ross to the terminal, and be there to pick him up when he returned. Other pilots envied Ross at being driven directly to the terminal instead of having to catch the crew bus from an outlying employee parking lot. The flight attendants that enjoyed this same benefit, being picked up by a boyfriend or husband, called this "princess parking." Ross would jokingly boast to his co-workers that he had "knight in shining armor" parking.

Ross was enjoying being assigned to the flight test department because it normally involved only out and back flights, called "turns," whereby Ross could be home every night.

Ross and Mary were pleased that today's test flight had been cancelled and they could spend the day together, even though the fog prohibited driving anywhere. All San Francisco transportation was at a standstill. They had just finished breakfast when Mary walked to the kitchen to answer the phone.

"It's for you, honey. It's Sam Pickering."

"What? Are you sure?"

Sam Pickering, President of Pacific Airlines, had never telephoned the Powers home before. Ross was surprised to hear his voice.

"Ross, we need you to fly to Anchorage today."

"But Sir," Ross offered, "This fog has closed the airport. Nothing is getting in or out of the Bay area today."

"I know Ross," Pickering said, "but, we've got the one aircraft equipped with HUD II and you're the only pilot trained in it!"

"That's correct, sir," Ross replied, "But the F.A.A. has still not certified it for passengers."

"Ross, I want you to listen carefully," Pickering went on.

"This morning I personally received special authorization from the F.A.A. to conduct one passenger operation, Flight 571 to Anchorage. This flight must depart within two hours!"

Ross was very surprised at this. In his thirty years of aviation experience he had never heard of such a thing. Receiving any authorization from the F.A.A. was a painstakingly slow process, let alone "special" authorization for technology not yet approved.

However, Ross accepted the situation, at a loss as to any reason to refuse the trip. This was new territory, one he was not well versed in.

"Sir, I live close to the airport but I am not sure I can even drive to the airport in this fog."

"Don't worry, Ross. We've made special arrangements with County Police to escort you to the airport in their vehicles. They can dispel fog with special lights, I'm told. The rest of your crew is likewise being transported. They will pick you up in fifteen minutes. You're the only pilot who can fly this thing, Ross. We're counting on you!"

It didn't immediately dawn on Ross to wonder what was so special about this one flight that would involve so many exceptional details.

In a few hours he would know.

"Dad, where are you going?" It was Draper, Ross and Mary's fifteen-year-old son.

"Got a special flight to Anchorage, should be home tomorrow. Wanna go?"

Ross loved to take family members on his trips when passenger loads would permit. He assumed today's flight would not be full.

"Sure, Dad," Draper happily replied, "no school today because of the fog!"

Minutes later:

"ID Badge?"

"Got it!"

"Hat?"

"Check!"

"Flight Bag?"

"Check!"

Ross and Mary enjoyed this last minute checklist exchange between them. It had become a loving last minute tradition before Ross would leave the house.

"Kiss?"

"You got it," as Ross would lean forward and kiss Mary. He was never to leave the house without that being the last item on that checklist.

The policeman at the door seemed momentarily surprised at the presence of the young boy. He had been directed to pick up only an airline captain for the fog-busting drive in the special vehicle.

Chapter 3   Oakland, CA

The beautiful sleek Lear Jet streaked across the sky. It was white with two flowing burgundy stripes that fanned to the rear forming a design that looked like an eagle's wings. Two perfectly symmetric cylindrical contrails followed the small jet as it sped at Mach .92, just below the speed of sound. In the small pilot's compartment were Brett Logan in the left seat and Tim Johnson in the right co-pilot seat.

The only passenger was Dr. David Bell He was dressed in his normal black slacks, black turtleneck, black sport-coat, and black lift-inserted shoes. He sat in the rearmost soft leather tan seat sipping white Chablis from the crystal glass just handed him by his personal flight attendant, a twenty-four year old blond beauty that was well paid for her "various" in-flight services.

Jet Charters, Inc. operated out of the small Northern California City of Redding. It was always available to transport him. Without that luxury his travels would not be nearly so convenient since the only airline to serve his hometown was a small commuter. He had depended so much on this small charter company, with a fleet of three aircraft, a Lear Jet 35, a Cessna Citation, and one turbo-prop powered Beechcraft King Air, that he bought the company the previous year. He knew very little about airplanes and left the management of the company and aircraft to others.

They had considered purchasing an aircraft with more than the one thousand mile range of either of the two jets. However, the limited range still allowed the frequently traveling doctor non-stop access from San Diego to San Francisco, and San Francisco to Denver. If his travel plans required longer distances he would simply be flown to a major city, where he would board a long distance flight. Such was the case for this flight.

He was ultimately bound for Anchorage, Alaska. However, it was necessary to take the Lear Jet to San Francisco the evening before so he could catch the very special flight to Anchorage in the morning. This flight would be aboard Air Force One as a guest of the President of the United States. As the small jet approached San Francisco a thick blanket of fog began to move into the area. It resulted in the visibility at San Francisco falling below that required by the jet, which was adequately instrumented for most IFR (Instrument Flight Rules) conditions. However, it lacked the state-of-the-art navigational capabilities, which would have allowed them to land in lower visibility conditions.

"November Seven One Two One Charlie Echo, this is San Francisco Center."

"Go ahead, this is Two One Charlie Echo." Once the initial contact is made, only the last two numbers, along with the letter designation is required.

"November Two Seven Romeo, the San Francisco weather is reported as winds calm, sky obscured, visibility one-eighth mile."

"Roger, that's too low for us. What is Oakland reporting?"

"Oakland is reporting visibility of two miles."

"Okay, we'll take an ILS approach into Oakland."

"Right, fly present heading, and contact Oakland Approach Control on 124.7."

Captain Brett turned around in his seat to face the cabin. "Dr. Bell, we can't get into San Francisco due to the fog. However, we can get into Oakland, about twenty miles away."

"Okay, have the airport arrange a limo for me to take me to San Francisco upon our landing."

"Yes Sir!"

After landing, the Lear Jet taxied to Flightcraft Aviation, one of several companies on the airport that cater to arriving and departing corporate jets. They also provide re-supply and refuel services.

Flightcraft had arranged for the long black Cadillac limousine within minutes of the radio call from the Lear Jet. It was ready as the jet pulled onto the ramp. With eighteen-inch wands, each encasing lit flashlights, the neatly uniformed ramp controller guided the Lear to a stop, just where its passenger door would open to a red carpet. At the other end of the carpet the right rear door of the black limo stood opened, in the control of the tuxedoed driver, who stood erect and at attention.

The co-pilot had left his seat and gone to the Lear Jet's door before the aircraft came to a complete stop. As the engines spooled down, the door was opened. Dr. David Bell, with not so much as one word, stepped out of the plane, and into the waiting limo.

The limo arrived at the hotel at 9:30 P.M., one hour and ten minutes after picking up its passenger. The fog had caused the traffic from Oakland to San Francisco to slow to a crawl. The hotel's doorman opened the rear door allowing a miffed and impatient passenger, who had been grumbling at the delay, to emerge. Again, without a word, or a tip, Dr. Bell proceeded to the front desk.

The Doubletree Hotel was situated within walking distance to the terminal at San Francisco. It is a vast complex with three story buildings spreading out in four directions. One tower stood at the center with twenty stories of rooms. The buildings reflected the ambiance of the Bay Area with wood buildings, trees galore, and perfectly placed man-made ponds.

After a short check-in procedure Dr. Bell entered his luxuriously appointed two-room suite on the twentieth floor. He walked directly to the bedroom's large picture window which faced toward the airport. He pulled open the drapes. The view that greeted him was something he'd never seen before.

Room 2004 was above the top of the fog level. The fog was laying on everything below, including the streetlights, airport terminal, and other buildings. However, the lights below could be seen through the translucence of the fog and provided and eerie, but beautiful, glow from below. Combined with the brightness of stars above the scene would have captivated most anyone who witnessed it. In-fact, many hotel guests on that side of the hotel's tower section had been mesmerized by it. Not Dr. David Bell.

The nation's leading authority on Late Term Abortions couldn't have cared less about the view. He abruptly closed the drapes and noticed that the phone message light was blinking. He picked up the phone and pressed the "message waiting" button.

It was Paula Graves of National Order of Feminists (NOF). "Hello, Dr. Bell, Paula Graves here."

There were no niceties - she sounded entirely businesslike. "Call me in room 615 when you get in. We need to discuss the Erica Paige situation."

Dr. David Bell and Paula Graves were in San Francisco for one reason, to meet up with and ensure that Erica Paige would accompany them to Anchorage tomorrow aboard Air Force One. And, since the 8 and ½ month pregnant San Francisco native had begun to express doubts about having the Late Term Abortion, it was up to Dr. Bell and Ms. Graves to come to San Francisco the night before the scheduled flight and personally ensure her cooperation.

Too much political weight rested on this one woman who would travel to Anchorage to become the first woman to receive the procedure. This would set the stage for other similar clinics to be established within well-reputed major hospitals instead of stand-alone clinics. Her plight of having to travel to Alaska for this procedure would be highly publicized and prepare the way for easier access to LTA's.

Bell punched 7 on the dial, followed by 615.

"Hello, Paula, I just got in. Made it just before the fog settled in."

"Yeah, I got in from Los Angeles several hours earlier. Doctor, I'm glad you're here. I've been in touch with Erica."

"Are there any problems?"

She continued, "I think it's all going to work out fine. She was still somewhat reluctant, but I convinced her that her abortion was dreadfully important, especially for the future of abortion rights."

Paula Graves was obviously proud of herself for the accomplishment.

"Excellent, Paula, what are the arrangements for tomorrow?"

He knew them but thought he'd give her more opportunity to shine.

Paula was happy to demonstrate her handle on the events, as they were to unfold.

"Erica is to meet us at the terminal at 11:15 A.M. Air Force One is scheduled to land at 2:00 P.M."

Dr. David Bell, NOF Vice President Paula Graves, and a young pregnant woman, Erica Paige, were all scheduled to be picked up in San Francisco by the President of the United States, James Jenson. It was a remarkable set of circumstances.

The President's airplane, Air Force One, was making an out-of-the-way stop in San Francisco while ultimately bound for Anchorage. The opening of a clinic specializing in LTA's, Late Term Abortions, was the catalyst for this very unusual schedule of activity, especially for someone like President Jenson.

"They want us to be ready to board the aircraft as it taxis in," Graves continued,

"Apparently, they won't even shut down the engines as we are boarded, followed by the immediate departure to Anchorage."

"Okay," Bell responded, now somewhat bored with hearing something he already knew, "I'll see you in the lobby, say about 8:00 A.M."

"Goodnight." Paula was somewhat put out by how uninterested Bell was in continuing the discussion.

Chapter 4   Washington, D.C.

The lights of the nation's capitol buildings gave Master Sergeant Joe Willis, Jr. goose-bumps each time he saw them. Even the 4:00 AM drive from his home in Silver Spring to his job at Andrews Air Force Base was enjoyable to him. Highly patriotic, Joe loved living and working near this most historic city. His home was located just north of the Washington D.C. border, at the corner of East-West Highway and Georgia Avenue. Even though Andrews Air Force Base was also located in Maryland, they were on opposite ends of the city, Silver Spring to the northwest, Andrews to the southeast.

It was a forty-five minute drive without traffic which was normally non-existent during his typical drive time. Most of his co-workers preferred to live nearer to the base; but, Joe's early morning drive through the city fed his patriotic spirit. He had inherited the home as the only child of Joe Willis, Sr., who had also served previous Presidents as caretaker of the Presidential airplane, Air Force One. Joe loved this city, and was occasionally called upon to escort VIP's visiting Washington for the first time. He became known as an expert of the layout and historical design of the city.

He loved giving his typical speech from the driver's seat:

"The city's layout had been the vision of Pierre Charles L'Enfant, a French architect who had joined the Continental Army. In 1791, he was commissioned by George Washington to design and construct the city, which featured broad avenues radiating out from Capitol Hill, interrupted by a series of rectangular and circular parks, all overlaid with a rectangular grid pattern of streets. This was done to help defend the city from invading armies!"

Joe's route brought him down Sixteenth Ave to Pennsylvania Avenue, just a few yards from the White House, before crossing the South Capitol Street Bridge over the Anacostia River, into Maryland, and on into Andrews. He had made this route several times a week for the last three decades. He had established the habit of casting a casual salute to the White House as he drove by. Several Presidents had received the unseen gesture of loyalty almost every morning of the week for the last thirty years.

However, for the last three years he had attempted to break the habit. It was difficult. He would find his right arm rising up as an automatic reflex as he passed by Sixteen Hundred Pennsylvania Avenue. He would catch himself before the saluting hand reached his forehead, and quickly place it back on the steering wheel. His opinion of the current President, James Jenson, was one of complete disdain. Consequently, today would be his last day on the job. Master Sergeant Joe Willis, Jr. was retiring.

He still drove the tug with the utmost care. The aircraft he was towing was Air Force One, a behemoth Boeing 747, which was much larger than the 707 that had been utilized by Presidents Eisenhower, Kennedy, Johnson, Nixon, Carter, Reagan, and Bush. This aircraft would be carrying the current sitting President, James Jenson, along with his wife, staff, and close friends.

President Eisenhower had been the first to make aircraft travel a vital part of the presidency. Before him, Truman and Roosevelt would have aircraft available but seldom used them. Eisenhower, however, had been an army general before becoming President and was therefore more confident in the safety of the relatively new technology. He loved aviation and was responsible for several aircraft being used for presidential travel. The first was a Lockheed Constellation, a 4-engine prop with a twin boom tail. First Lady Mamie Eisenhower had named that aircraft "Columbine," after the blue flower from Colorado, her home state. However, her fear of flying would keep her from enjoying the aircraft she had named. That aircraft was succeeded by the "Columbine II," a Super Constellation that was larger and faster than the original. Mrs. Eisenhower remained afraid to fly.

During the waning years of the Eisenhower administration jets were becoming popular. Two brand new Boeing 707s were ordered into Presidential service, one to fly the President, and one to fly the press.

In flight, while Air Traffic Control (ATC) was handling both jets, it had become somewhat confusing identifying which aircraft carried the president and which one carried the press. Controllers had been using the actual registration numbers for each jet as it flew, i.e. Boeing 200146 and 200147.

Colonel William Draper was President Eisenhower's pilot. During flight one day, and during some light confusion by ATC over the two aircraft identifications, Colonel Draper had an idea.

"Why don't you just call us Air Force One and Air Force Two?"

"Roger, Boeing 200... uh ...Air Force One. That's a great idea!"

ATC agreed and the names were established as they are to this day.

Now, the huge, shiny, two Boeing 747's are being readied for the Presidential entourage. The press will depart for Anchorage on Air Force Two three hours after Air Force One leaves. The reason for this is that Air Force One is scheduled to make a stop in San Francisco, while Air Force Two will fly direct to Anchorage.

At precisely 7:30 A.M. the Presidential entourage pulled onto the ramp. A few moments earlier the pilots had started engines three and four, both located on the right, non-boarding side of the huge aircraft. This President had insisted that he not wait on board for engines to start and taxiing to commence. He wanted the aircraft to begin moving as soon as he took his seat.

Air Force One would begin taxiing out with just the two engines running and then start the other two on their way to the runway. President Jenson looked at his watch as if to see how quickly they became airborne. If it weren't within eight minutes someone's head would roll. Air Force One lifted off six minutes after the President was seated.

The public address system aboard the 747 could be heard over the entire expanse of Air Force One. It was customary, even aboard the most important aircraft in the free world:

"Once again, Mr. President, welcome aboard."

It was a feminine voice, and a sexy one at that. It immediately got everyone's attention, especially that of the First Lady. It was the voice of the co-pilot.

"Our flight plan calls for a five and one-half hour flight to San Francisco, this morning. After a short stop to pick up our special guests in San Francisco, the continuing flight to Anchorage will take an additional five and one-half hours."

President Jenson was already irritated at having to make the trip in the first place. It was especially annoying that he was committed to make a stop in San Francisco to pick up the so-called "special guests." However, this was an extremely important political event. Besides, Mrs. Jenson had set the whole thing up. And he owed her...big-time!

She had invested most of her life to the attainment of the nation's highest office, something she always referred to as "their" Presidency. She was having a difficult time playing political games herself to keep "their" presidency from being destroyed by the scandals and escapades of her husband.

This trip to Anchorage could be the very event that would get things back on track. The continuation of this liberal presidency hinged, in her opinion, in the reaffirmation of his commitment to the feminist movement.

The National Organization of Feminists had threatened to remove their loyal support for President Jenson because of his highly public sexual scandals. The possible loss of NOF's support was the kiss of death for any liberal politician. President Jenson and his wife were not going to let that happen.

NOF promised to "look the other way" regarding Jenson's extramarital affairs if he would agree to be the keynote speaker at the opening of the nation's first "Late

Term Abortion" (LTA) clinic to operate within a large municipal hospital, Anchorage General.

Abortion rights had proven to be the most divisive issue facing this nation since slavery. This President had become the abortion rights advocate's flag bearer. Secretly, he loathed feminists. His sexual appetite determined his true opinions about the opposite sex.

His latest scandal involved sexual activity with a White House staff member. The "activity" had actually occurred in the Oval Office, and had nearly gotten him impeached. The support of the feminist movement, namely NOF, had saved this presidency before with threats and intimidation to Congressmen who were tempted to vote for impeachment.

Even aboard Air Force One he was secretly fantasizing about having sex with the co-pilot of Air Force One, a beautiful, black, Air Force Major that had obtained the job "expeditiously" after a Presidential recommendation.

Today would be the first day that Mrs. Jenson would actually see the lovely pilot. It would therefore be Major Victoria Speer's last flight as a crewmember aboard Air Force One. One word from the powerful First Lady and Major Speer's career was destroyed.

It wasn't that Mrs. Jenson was jealous. In fact, she could not have cared less on a personal basis. Her goal, however, was to prevent any further scandals that could possibly harm her own political aspirations, just one of which involved being the First Lady.

Secretly, she entertained ideas of holding political office, herself. Not just any political office. She thought of herself to be the future logical choice for the nation's first female president.

At his wife's urging, the President began to familiarize himself with the bios of the people that would be boarding Air Force One in San Francisco. He examined the list:

Dr. David Bell: The inventive physician who developed and perfected the procedures and instruments utilized in Late Term Abortions.

Ms. Paula Graves: Executive Vice President of NOF. A former Miss America.

Ms. Erica Paige: One of three women scheduled to receive an LTA, and the only woman traveling to Anchorage from another state.

The knock at the door of the Presidential Suite had urgency attached to it.

"Come In," the President said.

Mrs. Jenson looked up from the note she was drafting to the Commander of Andrews Air Force Base.

Mr. Jim Waters, Appointments Assistant to the Chief of Staff, George Evans, entered.

"Mr. President, we have a development, sir."

"Go ahead, Let's hear it."

"San Francisco is completely fogged in. The aircraft commander has informed me that a landing in San Francisco is impossible, and will most likely remain so for several hours, if not days."

"How could this happen?" the President was now angry. "Don't we have forecasts that would have let us know beforehand?"

"Yes Sir, but this fog bank had not been predicted. It has the entire San Francisco area in turmoil. Even auto traffic is at a standstill!"

The First Lady spoke affirmatively, "But it is imperative we land at San Francisco. There are three dignitaries that must ride with us to Anchorage."

"I'm sorry, Ma'am. There doesn't seem much we can do about it. Even as technologically advanced as Air Force One is, we can't land in zero visibility. It would not be safe."

The word "safe" seemed to placate her for a few minutes. "Then we will need for them to get on another airplane and meet us in Anchorage."

"I'm sorry, Ma'am." The aide was really nervous now. "I've been told by the pilot that no planes are departing San Francisco as well."

The President came up with a plan immediately. It was this quick thinking that allowed him to smoothly handle most any crises

"Get me Secretary Miller on the phone, now!"

Bob Miller is the Secretary of Transportation, which is over the Federal Aviation Administration, which has oversight of Pacific Airlines. Within five minutes the President is advised that Secretary Miller is on the special aircraft telephone.

"Bob, how are you?"

"Fine, Mr. President. How can I be of service?"

"I need to get some people from San Francisco to Anchorage, today."

"There is an airline in San Francisco, Pacific Airlines. But the news is reporting that San Francisco is fogged in."

"I know that, Bob. Now, do whatever you must do to get an aircraft off the ground and on to Anchorage."

"Yes, Sir. I'll get it done."

"I'll give you to my aide and he will give you the names of the three dignitaries that must be on that plane."

With that the President nodded to the aide to pick up the phone in another compartment, hung up, and leaned back, confident that all was taken care of. It was!

Dr. Bell and Paula Graves had met several times before. However, that didn't prevent Bell from being initially and instantly struck by her incredible beauty each and every time they met. It would only take a few seconds for him to return to reality, however. Once Paula Graves began talking, her radical militant feminism overrode the pleasure generated by an awesome physical presence.

Paula Graves stood five-foot seven inches tall, with medium length thick black hair, and a full-bodied figure that still brought much attention her way. She took many by surprise when they found out she was a member of NOF. She just didn't look the part. Her voice and mannerisms did, however.

"Good morning, Doctor. I hope you're well rested."

"Good morning, Paula."

Paula was smiling broadly, "Are you ready for our flight aboard Air Force One?"

When Paula smiled, it caused those who knew her well to be suspicious. Her smiles were usually only present when things were going exactly her way, which normally involved something with a diabolical twist. Dr.

David Bell had learned this over the years, but was always willing to meet with a representative of an organization that was militantly supportive of something that was making him millions of dollars per year.

"Yes," he was more formal now. "It's good that our President has put such importance on this event."

"Well, you can thank me for this opportunity," she bragged,

"Getting our "beloved President to go out of his way took some doing."

The word "beloved" had an interesting emphasis to it. Dr. Bell decided to let it pass without inquiry. Then, looking out through the window,

"By the way, look outside."

The fog was so thick that neither of them could see the shrubbery outside the window.

"This weather better not affect our plans," she worried.

"I shouldn't think so. It should probably burn off before noon," he said mistakenly. "Let's have breakfast."

Dr. Bell, as the owner of a jet charter company, was aware that a low layer fog bank could burn off from the top with the heat of the unobstructed sun from above. Fog would occur during meteorological conditions whereby the outside air temperature equaled that of the dew point, the calculated temperature at which the air begins to condense. Therefore, as the sun rises higher, and the heat from it increases, the air temperature would normally rise above that of the dew point, beginning a gradual dissipation of the fog. Sometimes, however, the fog would be too thick to dissipate completely, and would continue to hamper airport operations. Today's fog would not dissipate.

The two individuals walked into the restaurant and were directed to a table by the window.

"I hope you and the Mrs. enjoy breakfast," the hostess said.

Dr. Bell was content to let the mistake pass.

Paula Graves was not. A scene was in order.

"What makes you think you're smart enough to know what people's relationships are?"

Paula had now built up a frenzy to what Dr. Bell had determined was a meaningless event.

"Paula, I'm sure she meant nothing by it."

"I just don't like people assuming something about me that isn't true.".

She again turned to the hostess:

"What do you think? That I'm some submissive little housewife, here having breakfast with the man of the house?"

The hostess was now tearing up. She had never been spoken to that way after such an innocent statement.

"I'm sorry. Ma'am, it won't happen again."

"Make sure it doesn't," Paula was pointing fingers now. "Now, send the waitress over here, I'm ready to order!"

Dr. Bell decided to act as if he hadn't heard a thing. When the waitress arrived, nervous at having been briefed by the young hostess, the doctor ordered an omelet.

"I'll have a half grapefruit," Paula went on, "a fresh grapefruit. And you can warm my coffee up."

Just as they were finishing their breakfast the hotel manager approached. David suspected it had something to do with the treatment of the hostess. It was not.

"Are you Ms Graves?"

"Yes I am, and who the hell are you?" She too was expecting a fight.

"Ma'am, I'm the Hotel Manager. There is an urgent call for you."

"Oh, okay. Where can I take it?"

"In my office, ma'am, just inside the lobby."

As Graves stood up, she looked back at Bell.

"There better not be any more problems with this Paige girl!" Her true opinions were surfacing, "I'm getting a little tired of her attitude."

She returned after 15 minutes.

"Well, some things have changed."

"What's up," asked the doctor?

"It seems Air Force One cannot land here because of this stupid fog," she complained.

"We will be flying commercial to Anchorage."

"Well, I can't imagine, if Air Force One can't get in, that anything is operating at all?" Dr. Bell said.

"Yeah! Well, what the hell. All I know is that the Police will pick us up in thirty minutes to take us straight to the commercial jet. We won't even have to go through the terminal, at least."

"Do you know what flight we're going on? We have no tickets!"

"Well, I asked them that. They said we won't need any tickets. It's all taken care of. We're flying on Pacific Airlines Flight 571."

"What about the Paige girl?" Dr. Bell wondered.

"She is being picked up as well and is to be driven to the airport to meet us there." They were both obviously disappointed at not riding up on Air Force One. Perhaps, they wondered, they could return on the Presidential aircraft.

Chapter 5   San Francisco Intl. Airport

Captain Ross Powers and his son entered the terminal at 11:45 a.m.   It was packed with people, some of which had been marooned there since the night before.

Draper wondered, "Dad, how did all these people get here in the fog?"

"They've probably been here since yesterday." Ross responded.

He continued, "Stuck here all night, they look like they've slept on the floor. I wonder how many have been trying to get to Anchorage."

The sight of a uniformed pilot implied to the hundreds of people crowded in the Pacific gate area that a flight was soon to depart. Everyone wanted to know the destination.

"We're flying to Anchorage," Ross offered.

When it was discovered that only one flight would leave, and that one for Anchorage, there was a great moan of disappointment, except for the eighteen people that had been trying to get to Anchorage since late the night before. All of the others wanted other destinations and were quite upset that only one plane was going to depart, and, it was heading in the wrong direction. Most were headed to southern destinations, Los Angeles, San Diego, etc. The passengers heading for Anchorage were elated.

The Anchorage passengers were all going to be accommodated. They and three special people who were on the way to the terminal in police vehicles equipped with special lights.

"Captain, this is a real mess. Everyone wants to go somewhere and this flight to Anchorage is the only game in town," said the frantic gate agent.

"Well, at least we're getting one out."

"But the problem is that there are only eighteen of this mob that are headed to Anchorage," said the agent. Our last flight out last night got most Anchorage passengers out."

"Did it go out full?"

"Yeah, we just had these eighteen that got bumped. They've been sleeping in the terminal, or just up all night. It's been a real mess."

The agent looked around at the mob of people again.

"The company should use this one departing aircraft to go somewhere where most of these folks want to go!"

Not giving Ross a moment to respond,

"What's more, there are three supposed VIPs that are due here any moment. We have been instructed not to depart until they are on the plane."

Ross finally got a word in, "Sorry, wish I could help; but, I've got a plane to get ready for the flight."

Ross acknowledged the agent's problems, offered a conciliatory smile, a pat on the shoulder, and walked to the jetway door. His mind was only on the flight. What took place on this side of the jetway was completely out of his control.

In earlier days of aviation the captain had much more say in the entire operation of the flight, including issues involving passengers. It was not unusual for a captain to be called upon to solve disputes involving passenger boarding, lack of meals, etc.

The command authority of the captain over the years had been removed to the point that it only involved the actual manipulation of the controls, and safety decisions in flight. This new environment was difficult for older pilots who felt responsible for everyone, and did their best at ensuring that all aspects of the flight proceeded normally.

Others were now charged with those decision-making processes.

It was then, as he looked out the window at the aircraft parked at gate G6 that he noticed that his co-pilot today would be none other than Damien Pearce. Ross was immediately disappointed.

"Oh no, not him!" Ross muttered to himself.

Most captains did not like to fly with First Officer Pearce. There was just something about flying with him in that small cubicle of a cockpit that troubled them. It was that attitude! He was the cockiest pilot in the airline, with the least reason for being so. First Officer Pearce was a weak pilot. His skills were barely enough to get him through training. He was one who slipped through the cracks and managed to pass his yearly checks with the minimum passing grades.

Captain Ross Powers and First Officer Damien Pearce kept the cockpit door open as eighteen coach passengers boarded. With those eighteen, Draper Powers, and the three VIP's, the 136-passenger jet would be carrying only twenty-two total passengers.

"What a waste!" Ross mumbled as he silently approved of the agent's suggestion that a different destination should be used for this one operating flight.

Many other passengers with reservations never made it to the airport due to the fog. He noticed, barely through the fog, two police vehicles approaching the aircraft. They stopped and discharged three individuals.

"These must be the VIP's," Ross muttered. "Whoever they are, they're so important that they didn't even have to clear security."

Ross may have just as well been talking to himself.

First Officer Pearce was not even listening. Momentarily, he seemed totally preoccupied with something deep on his mind.

Dr. David Bell and Paula Graves were seated in the second row of First Class, across the aisle from each other, both occupying window seats. They were the only First Class passengers today. There had been a few more scheduled to fly First Class, but Paula Graves had seen to it that they were conveniently bumped to coach. The Airline complied. They didn't know exactly who this person was, but the President had set this whole thing up. Not the President of the Airline, it was the President of the United States.

Erica Paige had been seated in coach, at seat 8C. Paula had seen to this. She had no desire to lessen the First Class ambiance with that of someone like Erica. Erica was only useful to Paula for political purposes.

Damien had completed the exterior walk-around earlier and was now in his seat accomplishing his "flow," an activity that precedes the reading of the "Before Start Checklist," in which the actual items in the cockpit are checked and set. Ross was completing his flow from the left seat.

The dispatcher had previously filed a "canned" flight plan of the route. It was now time to obtain the actual route and altitude clearance from the control tower. It is the first officer's role to call "clearance delivery" on the VHF#1 radio while the captain listens and acknowledges.

"San Francisco Clearance, Pacific 571 to Anchorage, gate G12." The tower wanted to know where the flights were parked so that the upcoming taxi could be coordinated with "ground control."

"Pacific 571, you're cleared to Anchorage via the San Francisco Two Departure, as filed. Climb and maintain niner thousand, expect flight level three one zero within ten minutes. Departure frequency 120.4, squawk 4752."

"Squawk 4752." Reading back just the transponder code signified that you received and understood the entire clearance. In the old days the entire clearance would have to be read back. Crowded airports produced brevity in the read back procedure. Some final setting and checking of flight instruments and the "Before Start Checklist" is next. The first officer normally reads these query items of the checklist, and the captain does the responses, which have to be exact.

"Preflight?"
"Complete."
"Gear Lever & Lights."
"Down and Three Green."
"Oxygen & Interphone?"
"Checked."
"Fuel?"

"Thirty thousand pounds."

"Hydraulics?"

And on they would read and respond till the entire checklist was complete. There were checklists at every separate phase of a flight: Before Start...After Start...Prior To Push...Taxi...Before Takeoff...After Takeoff...Climb Through 18,000'...Descent...Approach...Before Landing...After Landing...and, finally, Shutdown.

Ross Powers was as comfortable at the controls of this jet aircraft as he was driving the family car - maybe more so. Actually, his desire to become a professional pilot didn't begin until he was 21 years old. He still jokes about his first airplane ride, just after graduating from high school, aboard a Central Airlines DC3 from his hometown of Martinsburg, West Virginia, to Washington D.C. on a hot bumpy day.

"It was a twenty minute flight and I had my head in a bag for eighteen of them."

He laughed every time he recalled the story.

Two years later, Ross saw an article in the local newspaper advertising a special five-dollar introductory flight in a Cessna 150. Having forgotten the previous bout of airsickness, he drove out to the airfield for his first flight in a small airplane. It was a beautiful calm day as the flight instructor, as an enticement, invited Ross to make the takeoff himself. Ross jumped at the chance and, with the flight instructor giving directions, flew the little airplane throughout the entire hour, including the landing.

Ross was hooked. At twenty-one, he knew exactly what he wanted to do for the rest of his life, fly airplanes. He had completed three years of college but decided to discontinue his formal education and devote his efforts to getting all the necessary licenses to become a professional airline pilot. He gathered as much information as he could from conversations with any airline pilot he could arrange to meet. He knew that the process would take years, but he was determined to make it through.

The first goal was to earn a Private Pilot's license. He had been so impressed with the flight instructor on the introductory flight that he arranged five lessons per week, at an hour each. Ross got a job as a aircraft fueler at the airport's flight training facility, which helped to lower the cost of the airplane rental. After ten hours of dual instruction it was time for Ross to solo. The first solo flight would be in the local flight pattern of the airport without straying out of the area. A student never knows when the instructor is going to let him fly solo, and looks forward to that moment excitedly.

Ross and his instructor had just landed and were taxiing back to the takeoff point when the instructor finally spoke the magic words:

"Ross, just drop me off by that fence over there. You take it around yourself!"

Young Ross tried to hide his excitement. This was a huge event in a beginning pilot's training. He brought the 150 to a stop.

"Okay, Ross, just do everything you've been doing. I'll be standing here, watching."

Ross released the brake and taxied to the takeoff point. After carefully checking to see if another airplane was on final approach, he pushed in the throttle to begin his takeoff. A Cessna 150 is just a two-seat airplane that is at or near its maximum weight with both seats occupied. Since the training till now there had been with two people in the plane, the little aircraft was handling significantly more powerful with only one in the airplane. It was exhilarating. As the 150 lifted off the runway, in much less takeoff distance than before, Ross began to almost laugh with joy.

"Actually," he would often say, "I laughed all the way around the pattern!"

The remainder of the training for the Private Pilot's license involved dual and solo cross-country flights. A minimum of forty hours of flight time is required before one is eligible for his flight test with a local F.A.A. Designee. Ross did a great job and, only eight weeks after his training began, he was awarded the first of many pilot licenses.

Ross would then earn his Commercial license, which required two hundred hours of flight experience, and some training for special maneuvers as well. An Instrument Rating, which authorizes the pilot to fly in the clouds without outside visual references, followed immediately. With these ratings Ross was duly licensed to work and be paid as a commercial pilot. His first job was with a local cargo carrying company, operating small single-engine and multi-engine aircraft. After eighteen months of employment, Ross had logged the necessary twelve hundred hours of flight time, which allowed him to begin training for the final, and ultimate pilot's license, the Airline Transport Pilot License.

Following the completion of that training and having earned his "ATP," Ross set off for higher ground. After six more months with a small commuter airline Ross was finally interviewed and hired as a co-pilot by Pacific Airlines, based in San Francisco.

On his second trip flying the Boeing 737-100 he met a lovely Flight Attendant, Mary Draper.

They were married within the year and soon had the first of four children. Mary gave up her life as a flight attendant, a decision that was initially very difficult. The airlines had offered to allow her to stay on leave as long as she desired, if only she would return some day. Mary declined and resigned. She had always envisioned herself as a stay-at-home mom, something she wished she could have had growing up herself. She was determined to be a full time mom for her future kids. Ross adored her for that; So did the children!

Now, at the age of 51, Ross Powers has been a pilot with Pacific for over 26 years, 16 of that as a captain. Two pilots are required in the 737, a captain, the pilot in command, and a first officer, or "co-pilot."

He has always had the reputation of a dedicated family man and respected pilot. It was never a priority for him to be known as an "Ace of the base" pilot, a nickname used for the hotshot guys who believed they were God's gift to aviation. Ross Powers wanted only to be as safe and as professional as he could be.

"There are 'old' pilots, and there are 'bold' pilots, but there are no 'old bold' pilots," he would often say.

The six foot, two inch tall, blue eyed, always smiling, people-person knew no strangers. He liked everyone he met and, as such, he loathed confrontation; it was just not natural for him. At times he wished to be more assertive, more authoritative. This wasn't part of his personality. He could argue, however, if forced too. At times in his life he has known some real "knock down drag out" conflicts. It was later, though, after the conflict, when

Ross, whether right or wrong in the controversy, would internally suffer, as if there was something deep in his nature that abhorred the coldness and anger that one person could direct to another.

Some thought him to be naïve at times. When a nationally known entertainment figure was acquitted by a jury for the stabbing death of his ex-wife, Ross was the only one among his acquaintances to agree with the verdict.

It was this sensitivity, however, that made him receptive to any proponents of religion. He'd listen to anyone and examine whatever anyone had to say. He did not grow up in a religious family. In fact, his parents refused to discuss religion whenever it came up in a conversation, proclaiming their beliefs to be a "private" matter and no-one else's business, even their children.

Ross had questions. He always sought for the good in a person and therefore always sought for the good answer in any question, especially those about God. He often pondered about the origination of man and just stayed quiet and listened, waiting for the good answer, the right answer. The choices coming his way regarding the subject would have a qualifying or disqualifying character. If it didn't come across as "good" it would never even get to the "correct or incorrect" test in Ross's analysis.

It was the sum total of these attributes that prompted Ross, at age 26, to accept the message of a traveling evangelical troupe. It was explained to him that Jesus was actually the Son of God, and had died for Ross, paving the way to heaven for him. It hadn't actually been easy. Ross held back for a while and it was getting late in the evening. However, the message was one that contained so much good; that God was so good to have provided his own son for Ross's benefit.

The meeting around a hotel pool was getting ready to break up when a local pastor said to him, "Ross, perhaps this is not the night for you."

He continued, "I can see that you are taking this decision very seriously. That's good."

"I know, but can't we just go on for a little bit longer?"

"Ross, everyone here is exhausted."

There had been several in the group that had accepted the Lord that evening. Ross was the last holdout. All of the ones not interested had long since left. The rest just sat and prayed that Ross would just go ahead and receive the Lord, so everyone else could just go to bed. They all knew he would eventually come. If not tonight, then maybe tomorrow. His heart was obviously touched by the message.

"Ross," the man said, "Let's just bring this to a close for tonight. We can talk more tomorrow. All I ask you to do just now is pray with me The Lord's Prayer."

"Okay," Ross quietly replied.

And then, the two men began to pray in unison, "Our Father, who art in heaven...."

It was all it took. Just then Ross fell over weeping to the floor. All bystanders ran to him and held him, placing their hands on him, praying...

They let him weep for over a minute.

Then, "Ross, God has prepared your heart to receive Him. Are you ready?"

"Yes," was all the Ross could say.

So there, at approximately 2:00 am in San Antonio, Texas, Ross Powers' faith became a principle that would affect every issue of his life, especially issues he'd face today as Captain of Pacific Flight 571.

By the time, however, that Ross started his job as a pilot for Pacific Airlines some years later he had slipped somewhat from the faith. He had been so focused on the beginning of his career that God had taken a back seat in his life. God was still important to him, but other things took a slightly higher priority.

In fact, when he first met and flipped head-over-heels for Mary he had been in a total back-slidden condition.

Their first home was a small condo in Southern California, where they were initially based with Pacific. Some neighbors invited Ross and Mary to a Wednesday night couples bible study. Unknown to the neighbors, Ross and Mary had been having marital troubles and they themselves were contemplating divorce. However, they had just discovered that Mary was pregnant.

This pregnancy was the glue that was keeping this troubled marriage together. Neither was happy about the possibility of being separated when the child would arrive.

During this bible study Ross was deep in thought. His heart was ready to burst with anguish over his back-slidden condition. He knew that, since life and marriage were in turmoil, only returning to Jesus was the answer.

He also figured that Mary had only dutifully sat and endured the one hour bible lesson. At its end, he said to Mary:

"Would you mind waiting up by the door? I'd like to speak with the pastor."

Mary, without a word, left the pews and moved to the back of the room by the doors. Ross continued to believe that she was terribly upset at having to wait even longer.

Ross walked up to the pastor and waited for some others to finish their conversation with him. His heart felt like bursting, as God had been moving mightily in his heart, to come back to him. As he approached the pastor,

"Pastor, I'm a back-slidden Christian, and…"

Before he could finish the sentence the pastor said abruptly:

"Where is your wife?"

"She's up by the door, but… but…"

"What's her name?"

"Mary, but…but…"

The pastor looked up towards the door and loudly said, "Mary, would you come here?"

Ross began to moan to himself, "This pastor doesn't know it, but he's about ready to ruin any chance of our marriage." He thought on, "Mary is really going to be upset about all this!"

When Mary arrived by the pastor the first words out of his mouth were:

"Mary, would you like to receive Jesus Christ as your Savior?"

All sound in this small chapel stopped.

Mary simply said, "Oh yes I would."

Ross was stunned to silence. He began to realize that, while God was working on his heart, He was working on Mary's as well.

The pastor led them both to the first row of pews. The other couples attending the study all came over behind us. Their hands were all gently touching Ross and Mary's shoulders. They were praying quietly.

The pastor then led Mary into that wonderful place where a person gives their life to Jesus Christ. She wept as if this moment had been long overdue. Her fears and heartaches were replaced with a sweet peace.

The pastor then turned to Ross.

"Ross, would you like to re-dedicated your life to The Lord?" He continued, "The Holy Spirit wishes to help you live for the Lord."

Then an invitation. "Would you like to ask the Holy Spirit to empower you to live for The Lord?"

"Yes, Pastor. I would."

Then, with the wonderful affirmation of all that stood with their hands on Ross and Mary, they both were led…

"Holy Spirit, fall on me as you did at Pentecost. We desire the same relationship with you as was spoken of in Acts 1."

Later that night, after going to bed, Ross asked Mary if she wanted to pray. She said "Yes" and they both got out and knelt by the bed. And, there on that slightly moonlit floor, Ross and Mary prayed together, hand in hand. Their real marriage began at that moment.

"Ground to flight deck,"

The lead ramp man was on the intercom radio, a communication link between a receptacle located on the lower part of the aircraft nose and the cockpit.

"…walk-around is complete and we're ready to push when you are."

Since the passengers were seated, the doors closed, the clearance to "push" was received from the tower.

Ross responded, "Roger, brakes are released, we're cleared for pushback."

The big jet began to move backwards.

After a few minutes of pushback the intercom once again from below, "Captain, you're cleared to start One and Two."

It was standard procedure to start the left engine, engine number one, first, followed by engine number two. This was because the baggage compartments are located on the right side of the aircraft. Starting engine number two last would give baggage loaders an extra opportunity to load a last minute bag if one showed up. It was not safe for baggage personnel to be around the baggage compartments with the right engine running.

The engines are started in a two-step process. First, the ignition switch is turned to the on position, which allows high-pressure air from an Auxiliary Power Unit

(APU) to begin spinning up the engine's compressor section. Then, after the spin-up shows a pre-determined percent, the fuel lever is raised, allowing fuel to enter the engine, causing combustion and light-off. The engine then continues to rotate to the idle power setting.

Engine #1 was started, followed by Engine #2.

"Set brakes," said the tug driver.

"Brakes are set, you're cleared to disconnect, see ya later," Ross replied.

"Have a good flight, Captain."

The "After Start" checklist was accomplished and Damien called Ground Control for permission to taxi.

"Pacific 571, as I'm sure you know, we are unable to see anything from the tower today. So, you're cleared to taxi, at your discretion, to Runway 16. No other aircraft are presently moving on the airport".

The crew had already known which runway was in use for takeoffs this morning. During the initial cockpit setup, the co-pilot had dialed in 118.0 on the number two radio. That was the frequency for "ATIS," Automatic Terminal Information Service. This provided the local meteorological situation at San Francisco at the time, as well as runway and general airport information helpful to outbound crews

The San Francisco ground controller understood well the legal significance of the words "…at your discretion," just communicated. Even though he could easily monitor the movement of the aircraft on ground radar it was procedure to shift all responsibility for safe movement onto the flight crew when visibility was so restricted. The tower would not even be able to see the aircraft takeoff.

The fog had blanketed the entire west coast. The closest areas of open airports were Los Angeles to the south and Anchorage to the north. This meant that Flight 571 could not return to San Francisco if an emergency developed during or shortly after takeoff. Crews were always trained for the worst possible scenario and today's flight had to go to Anchorage even if an engine failure occurred during the takeoff. Therefore, the aircraft was fueled to its capacity of 36,000 pounds, much more than normally required.

Ross Powers had been trained to handle any possible emergency situation. Except the one he would face today. No training could have prepared him for this.

Taxiing out in heavy fog was particularly difficult this day for Flight 571. From the cockpit of the 737 Ross could hardly make out the yellow taxi line that would guide him onto taxiway "B," and up to edge of Runway 16 Left. Fortunately, the Tower had turned all taxi lights up to their highest setting and was using their ground radar system to provide progressive taxi instructions to the pilots.

"Pacific 571, ya got a minute for a question?" It was the ground controller.

"Sure, go ahead," responded Ross.

The controller continued, "We've never experienced anyone taxiing out for takeoff in zero visibility. What gives?"

Ross had no real answer for them, "Oh, it seems the company was able to get some last minute approval for the use of this new technology that allows zero visibility takeoffs."

"That's peculiar," the controller continued, "normally they let us know about this kind of thing before it's actually used. We've been caught by surprise with this one."

"Me too!" Ross replied, "Me too!"

After a 25-minute taxi that normally required 10, the tower cleared the aircraft onto the runway.

"Pacific 571, you are now cleared for takeoff. Please advise when you are off the ground."

"Roger, tower, we are moving into position now on 16L." Damien was now working the radios. Ross was making the takeoff. Pilots would usually alternate legs. It was not unusual for the captain to fly the first leg of a trip and, especially in this case. Only the captain can perform a

HUD takeoff, because the viewing lens was only located on the left side

On the runway now Ross illuminated the inboard landing and runway turnoff lights. This was normal procedure for an aircraft cleared for takeoff. It served to let other aircraft waiting to taxi that this flight had been cleared for takeoff. This procedure resulted from the 1971 crash where two 747's collided on the ground. One was taking off, while the other was taxiing down the runway. It was the largest fatality count in aviation's history. Today, however, the lights were on in vain. No one could see them anyway.

As Ross brought the power up on the 22,000 pound thrust engines the 737 began to accelerate down the runway. With his eyes peering through the HUD Ross could easily maintain directional control down the center of the runway.

"80 knots," Damien stated as the airspeed indicator tape rolled down, "looking for 131."

131 was the speed, in knots, that represented "V1", the go/no go speed. Before "V1" a safe abort could take place. Beyond that speed, no matter what calamity might occur, including an engine failure or fire, the takeoff must be continued. The remaining runway length would be insufficient to stop.

The "V" referred to speed, originating from the word "velocity."

"V1" Damien stated while Ross removed his right hand from the throttles.

"Vr."

The "r" stood for "rotate." At Vr Ross would gently, but decisively, pull back to an attitude of about 22 degrees, indicated on the HSI, the horizontal situation indicator (formerly known as the artificial horizon).

As the nose of the 130,000 lb. aircraft pointed up, the entire aircraft would smoothly and majestically launch into the air. Pilots would often joke to non-fliers that flying was easy.

"Just pull back and the houses get smaller!"

The limited visibility prohibited any houses from being seen today. The takeoff was a complete instrument procedure, meaning no visual reference to the ground was utilized

The takeoff on runway 28L (there was a parallel runway, 28R) meant that the initial heading of the aircraft was a westerly 280 degrees. A turn to the north after five miles was instructed on the instrument departure chart, included in the initial clearance. Within 4 minutes the Boeing 737-800, with a crew of five, and a passenger load of just twenty-two passengers, had turned to a northwesterly heading and was well on its way for the 5 hr and 55 minute flight to Anchorage.

It would be the longest 5 hour and 55 minute flight ever known by any aboard Pacific Flight 571, crewmember or passenger.

Back in First Class Dr. Bell could see nothing but a blanket of fog from his window seat. He wondered how on earth they could taxi this aircraft in this terrible visibility. However, as a seasoned flyer he fully trusted the two guys up front to know what they were doing. After all, he had more important things on his mind.

Across the aisle, and at the opposite window seat, Paula Graves cared less about what was going on around her. She was used to getting her way. Not even the weather would prevent her from getting to Anchorage. If the pilots had not been able to handle the weather she reasoned she could have complained loudly enough to force the airline to get her some pilots who could.

Passing through 18,000 feet the three altimeters in the cockpit, captain's, first Officer's, and the standby, were set to 29.92. Below 18,000 feet all altimeters are set to the actual setting of barometric pressure reported nearest their location.

This allows all aircraft to be reading the same reference of flight altitude and prevent possible collisions. For instance, the San Francisco altimeter setting given by

ATIS information was 30.02. This equates to 30.02 inches of barometric pressure reported for the entire San Francisco area. This setting would suffice until the aircraft was far enough away and perhaps flying through a different barometric pressure system. In order to ensure that all aircraft were provided adequate vertical separation it was decided long ago that altimeters would be set to 29.92 at and above 18,000 feet in spite of what the actual barometric pressure might be at their geographic location.   Since all aircraft had the same setting at the higher altitudes they could be separated so as not to be flying at the same altitude as another in the same location. Aircraft flying below 18,000 feet must acquire altimeter settings as they move from one location to another.

"Ladies and Gentlemen, the captain has turned off the seat belt sign and we are about to serve dinner selections. Today, you have a choice between the chicken or the chicken." Flight attendant Michael Osteen always gave humorous PA's.

It never set well with his flying partner, Harold Otten. "Michael, you are such a twit!" Harold said as he crowded into the aft galley.

"Yeah, but you still love me," Michael replied as he squeezed up against his gay lover.

Michael and Harold would always fly together. Both were senior enough to bid the trips they wanted and did not attempt to hide from anyone, passengers included, the fact that they were an "item."

Harold Otten was thirty-one years old and had been a flight attendant with Pacific Airlines for seven years. He had initially wanted to be with an airline with a San Francisco crew domicile, but was grateful to land a job with Pacific, in spite of the fact that San Francisco was its only domicile.

Harold grew up in Burbank, California, the only child of wealthy parents, Robert and Susan Otten. He had many early childhood memories of loud and lavish parties that his parents hosted in their beautiful, large, six bedroom home. He was too young to question why a family of three would need so many bedrooms. As he grew older he understood perfectly.

The parties occurred weekly, sometimes twice a week. They would begin early in the evening, about 7:00 o'clock. Within a few hours there would inevitably be a steady stream of party participants heading for various bedrooms. Harold, who often sat peaking through the banisters, would quickly dash back into his room as the first sets of people headed up the stairway. Occasionally, when the bedrooms were full, some errant couple, desperate to find privacy, would enter Harold's bedroom by mistake, or just by being too drunk to care. Normally, the couple would recognize their error and immediately leave the room. However, a few times, the two people would land passionately on his bed, not knowing of Harold's presence. He would roll onto the floor where he could not be seen, and just listen. And sometimes, when the moon was full, he could actually watch…men with women, men with men, women with women.

Robert Otten was a movie producer. He didn't produce action films, family films, or comedies. He produced pornographic movies. For years, the family was quite removed from the day-to-day business of the father, who had originally gone to great strides to keep the Otten name from being associated with the films he was producing. However, the parties obliterated any anonymity he had otherwise desired. Cocaine use became the driving force, and the presence of a single child did not deter the activities.

In addition to observing the bedroom activities, young Harold, who enjoyed sneaking in to his parents' room and rummaging through their belongings, often discovered magazines and pictures that his father used to seek out new talent. Unbeknownst, even to his parents, eight year old Harold was developing an intense attraction to pornography. Over the years, that attraction would grow more specific, with Harold preferring to view pictures of males, rather than females. By the time he entered high school he was terribly conflicted about his own sexuality. He thought about sex all of the time, as if he viewed the world through a pornographic filter. He yearned for a defining experience that would determine, once and for all, his sexual preference.

That experience would come in his sophomore year at Burbank High School. Harold had enrolled, and excelled, in the Drama Class. It was at the end of a late evening rehearsal for the annual play.

"Harold, can I see you in my office?" It was Mark Robinson, the drama teacher, who had been watching Harold for months.

"Yes, Mr. Robinson, I'll be right there."

Harold had been picking up "vibes" from Mr. Robinson, and caught him staring often. He would return the stares in a flirtatious way and had been daydreaming about a rendezvous with the man twenty years his senior. Today, the rendezvous would occur.

When it all got started, back in the darkened office, it was unclear who the aggressor was. They were to meet there every day. Mark Robinson introduced his young protégé to other members of his favorite organization, AMBLA, America Man-Boy Love Association. Soon, Harold was deeply involved himself, and succeeded in recruiting many other high school males into the program.

Michael Osteen had always had what his family would call, "a tenderness." It seemed he was born with an effeminacy. It did not develop with age, it was not contrived, and it was as natural as brutishness was natural in a neighborhood bully. All throughout his young life he made friends easily.

Everyone liked Michael, and he went through high school as one of the most popular students. Athletes liked Michael, cheerleaders like Michael, even the school punks liked Michael. He was president of his Senior Class. No one gave a second thought to his feminine ways. It even added to what made him so likeable, so non-threatening. High School was the greatest time in Michael's life.

He had wished it could have gone on forever - but it didn't. When it was over, there were initially some opportunities for him to see and spend time with his high school friends. But soon, those times would diminish, then end entirely. Everyone had new lives, most with jobs or college. Michael would come home from college occasionally hoping to find some of his friends. It was over.

It's not quite certain how Michael ended up at San Francisco State College. It might have been a suggestion of a family friend, or the weather in the Bay area upon his first visit. Whatever it was, it was the worst possible place Michael could end up. While still a freshman, his desire for friendship would send him on a journey that would determine his sexual identity for the rest of his life.

Michael was not a homosexual in the true sense of the word. He did not desire sex with males. He did not desire sex with females. Michael just wasn't interested in sex at all. In college he was now in the midst of hundreds of fellow students who had no good friends. In that situation people are magnetized to others with similar characteristics.

The athletic type is drawn to others similar. The studious type ultimately ends up with a group of high intellectuals. Likewise the hippy, the cheerleader, the goof-off, and people like Michael. Michael's new friends were like him. This was so different from before when he had been the only one around with effeminate characteristics.

Michael never went into the proverbial closet. He was shoved into it without really desiring the lifestyle. Michael's new friends were introducing him to the gay world full of sex and a party atmosphere as that enjoyed by his old buddies from high school. Only these were different than high school parties- there were no girls there. None were needed.

Michael carried with him an internal conflict with this new life. However, after a few years that conflict would give way to a committed identity. He was gay. He was lonely, unfulfilled, and unhappy - but he was gay. Yet, in his secret thoughts, he remembered.

It was at one of the parties that he met Harold Otten.

"Hi, I'm Harold." Harold had made the first move.

"Hello, I'm Michael."

A smile, a playful glance, and this whirlwind relationship hit the ground running at about 100mph. It was an immediate attraction. Harold was drawn sexually toward Michael. Michael was in desperate need of a friend, a close friend. Becoming a pair was just something they both felt they were supposed to do. It was as if someone else were telling them what to do.

After the weekend, Harold and Michael would accompany each other to the interviews for flight attendants being conducted by Pacific Airlines in San Francisco.

Male flight attendants began to appear in great numbers during the 70's. While many of them are gay, a large percentage of them are straight, many of who have wives and children. It is, however, a comfortable environment for gay men, and female flight attendants seem to enjoy working with them. It was once explained that the women found friendships with gay men to be rewarding and comfortable, perhaps due to the absence of a normal draw to the opposite sex that would be lacking in these relationships.

Harold and Michael were a couple. They had committed themselves to a lifelong relationship that was to involve completely open sex, and completely open honesty. Both were keeping up their bargain on the sex issue. Only Michael was keeping up the "honesty" issue…Harold had never told him about the positive result from the test for HIV, the AIDS virus, which he had contracted before he had met Michael.

"Pardon me, may I get you a beverage?" Janie Stone always had a becoming smile on her face as she dealt with passengers. In fact, it was Janie's nature to be wonderful to every person she'd meet. She enjoyed the reputation of being the kind of Flight Attendant that made the flight a most pleasant one.

While some flight attendants received "onion letters" from complaining passengers, Pacific Airlines was continuously receiving "orchid letters" from passengers aboard Janie's flights. On Flight 571, she was working First Class, while Michael and Harold took care of coach.

"Yes, I'll just have coffee," said Dr. Bell.

"Scotch and Soda," demanded the woman in 2F.

Chapter 6 Redding, CA

David Bell had always known that he would be a physician. He felt it was his destiny. He chose the field of obstetrics and had been content treating pregnant women and delivering babies.

Happily married and the father of three children, two girls and a boy, he had become the Chief of Obstetrics at Redding Lutheran Hospital in this small Northern California town, which sat at the northern end of the Sacramento Valley. He most likely would have lived out the rest of his life, happy and pleased with his life there in Redding, until that night in Sacramento that changed his life forever.

Seven years earlier, Dr. David Bell, his wife, Betty, and their children, three under the age of 5, were returning from a ski trip to Lake Tahoe. They had rented a beautiful ski-in ski-out cabin on the slopes of Heavenly Valley.

David, at age thirty-five, was in top physical condition. At five-foot, ten inches tall, he weighed a perfect one hundred and fifty-five pounds. His dark hair and green eyes, along with striking, handsome features drew looks from women wherever he went.

Betty only minded it a little when women gawked. Secretly, she prided herself at her wonderful marriage to such a handsome man. She herself was extremely attractive. At thirty-four, she still looked good, even after having three children. She had long blond hair that came down to just above her shoulders, and then flipped up slightly. She had regained her figure and was still able to fit into the tight ski-clothes she had been wearing when she and David met, eight years earlier, on the slopes of Lake Tahoe's Heavenly Valley.

Betty's mother, who lived in Oakland, California, accompanied them, as she normally did on their ski trips, to care for the children in the cabin while David and Betty skied the days away. Now after four fun-filled days they were halfway home, exhausted, but exhilarated at the wonderful time they had been having.

The drive from Lake Tahoe to Redding would take them west on Highway 50, which wound through the Sierras, to Sacramento, where they would pick up Interstate Highway 5, north to Redding. It would normally be a two and one-half hour drive to Sacramento, and another three hours to Redding.

Highway 50 from Tahoe to Sacramento had been somewhat slow this evening due to slippery road conditions, especially at this hour of the evening, long after temperatures had dropped further than what they were earlier with the heat of the sun.

"Honey, that was the best vacation we've had in a long time." David was holding Betty's hand.

"I agree, everything went perfect, the snow was awesome, and the kids were extremely well-behaved. I'm sure glad Mom came with us to keep the kids occupied."

The children and Betty's mother were asleep in the back two seats of the large blue Chevrolet Suburban. Two pairs of skis, his Rosignols, and her K2's, were tightly locked into the ski rack above.

"Hey," said David, "I'm ready for a potty break. Should we wake the kids?"

"No, I don't think so. They're exhausted. Besides, they went just before we left Tahoe an hour and a half ago. They're fine. So am I."

David spotted the neon sign of a "Burger Barn" just ahead and on the right. It would be a quick and easy stop that should take only a few minutes. He pulled over into the parking lot, stopped the car alongside of a few others, and got out; leaving the engine running so the heater could remain on for the others.

There were only three patrons, two adults and one teenager, sitting at the tables, and only one attendant behind the counter. He walked by, hoping the attendant wouldn't notice a non-customer coming in to use the restroom. David had thought about ordering a hamburger to justify his presence, but couldn't bring himself to do it.

He loathed fast food. He didn't even want to even spend two dollars supporting the industry.

As he walked down a side hallway and into the restroom, he noticed a man drying his hands with a paper towel.

He took no note of the man's appearance, except for the knit hat he wore. David walked to one of the three urinals and breathed a loud sigh as relief came. He heard, but did not see, the other man come from the toilet stall. He had barely calculated that the first man was still there when things started to go black. The cold nylon arm of a sports jacket had him around the neck.

There was such initial confusion. Someone, perhaps two, had grabbed him, pulled him back, and were choking him. Barely conscious, he could feel them grope for his back pocket where he normally kept his wallet. It was in the car. He began to hear the profane anger that was directed to him. He couldn't understand why they were hurting him.

"Okay, dude, where's your money"?

He lessened the chokehold to get a response.

"I didn't bring it," David barely gasped, "I left it at home."

"You're lying." The chokehold was tighter

"Where is it, tell us, or I'll blow your head off right here!"

"No, really, I don't have it!"

David was in shock, but cognizant enough to attempt steering them away from thinking about going to the car.

"Where's your car? Which one is it? What color is it?"

"No, I didn't drive," He was desperate, still being choked.

"I got dropped off here, I'm...uh...uh waiting for a friend to pick me up."

David begged.

"Please," he pleaded, "stop hurting me, I don't have any money!"

The last thing David hazily heard was something about a plan to go search the parking lot for his car. Panic was already there, but now rose to the highest level.

"Let's kill him; he ain't got money on him."

David was totally powerless to fend off his attackers. Never before had he felt so helpless. He felt the blade of a knife pressed against his side. Then he felt it being replaced by a gun. There was a deafening shot, the sound of which he would never forget. Strangely, there was no pain, even though he knew he had been shot. There was only one thought - this life was over. As he fell to the floor he could see the tennis shoes of his attackers as they exited.

Fighting to maintain some semblance of his surroundings, he could feel the spread of blood, his blood, spreading over the floor of the restroom. Why was he still alive? He was beyond feeling pain and lay there, collecting what thoughts he could from fading consciousness, hopes of not bleeding to death. Then he thought about his family, and the danger they might be in. He desperately tried to crawl to the door, in hopes of summoning help. He had to get someone to go outside to prevent an attack on his family. He faded, and then passed out completely.

The three patrons in the restaurant, and the attendant had not even recognized the sound of the shot. They had determined that it had only been the backfire of a passing vehicle. David Bell was near death on the rest-room floor. He would have surely died had it not been for the young boy's need to urinate. He had been sitting with his parents at one of the tables and was now entering the rest room, almost slipping in the crimson pool of blood that covered the floor. Within minutes, David Bell was being attended too by one of two Sacramento Police officers who had been driving by, when flagged down by the father of the young boy who had found David.

David didn't find out until much later that his robbers had been frightened off in the parking lot when the man ran out, screaming for help. A police vehicle was driving by, and the muggers took off running. They were captured within the hour.

The light was as bright as the sun. He couldn't squint...didn't want to. David Bell was emerging from fifteen hours of unconsciousness and was slowly becoming aware of his surroundings.

"I must be dead," he thought. "This is not so bad."

The light above the bed was pointed straight down into his eyes. It was all he could see. Then, he began to hear a clacking sound that had some cadence to it. It grew louder and louder as the light grew brighter. Awareness was in a battle with fuzziness, that brief time just before regaining consciousness. The roaring, rhythmic, clacking sounds slowly became distinguishable, more like voices. The light shrunk to a specific glow that came from the fixture above.

Then, he was awake. His first memory, before even speaking, was the previous thought that he was dead. Now, surprisingly, there were faces looking down on him, one very familiar. It was Betty.

"Hi, Darling." Her voice was soothing, encouraging.

Then, another voice, from the other side of the bed.

"You're lucky to be alive, sir. One more inch and you would have been a statistic!"

"Betty, is everyone okay? Did those guys get to you?"

"No, Honey, we never even saw them."

"Did they catch them?"

"Oh yes! They should be in jail for a long time."

The recovery process was long and arduous, hampered in part by the failure to sleep. Sleep brought those nightmares. The attack would happen night after night in David's dreams until he fought to stay awake. Time would allow the knife wounds and choke damage to heal, but David had been changed forever.

The trial was postponed until David had recovered enough to testify. He was brought into the courtroom in a wheelchair, sworn in, and assisted to the witness stand. He sat in the witness box staring at the two men, looking to be in their early twenty's, and was incredulous at their smug, cocky, attitudes. They were sitting at the defendants' table cracking smiles. As David spoke, they would snicker in disdain.

"Has the jury reached a verdict?"

"We have, Your Honor."

"You may announce your verdict."

Betty squeezed David's hand as if to say that it was all going to work out fine.

"We find the defendants not guilty."

David felt a bolt go through him as if shot out of a cannon. There was shock all around him. He couldn't speak. Neither could Betty.

"Mr. Giles and Mr. Johnson, you are hereby released."

David watched as the two gave themselves "high fives." They turned immediately and looked directly into David's eyes. Simultaneously, they pointed at him, as if to threaten him further. The judge and the jury were making their way out of the courtroom. One of the jury witnessed the threatening gesture and just shook his head. The two men, who had moments ago been faced with an Attempted Murder charge with a possible sentence of twenty years, walked by, sneering at their wheel chaired victim.

"See you a Burger Barn, Chump," one of them said.

"Hey, is this the woman you were with that night? Man, we could've had fun with her," said the other as they continued out the door.

David and Betty waited in silence as the entire courtroom emptied. They were in shock.

David Bell would never be the same. He became moody and introverted, and for months, refused to even go outside his home. He would have occasional fits of rage, even at the three small children. As time went on, he got worse.

There would be counseling at first; then psychiatric evaluation.

"David, darling. We have got to fix this. I feel us drifting apart." Betty had been fretting over this since David was released from the hospital ten weeks earlier.

"Betty, I'm fine. I just need some time to sort things out." He had started out somewhat conciliatory, but had instantly turned angry.

"If you don't like being married to me, than you know what you can do!"

Betty would never really know him again. She hoped that David would return to his former self but it was never to happen. The outbursts of rage had become more frequent, and more violent, and she was beginning to fear for her safety, and that of the children.

Returning to his practice, David began to deliver babies again. It was different now. He had begun to see the faces of the muggers in the faces of newborns he was delivering. He was becoming more and more emotionally, and mentally, incapable of separating normal life from the horrible events of that night in Sacramento.

David sought counseling. Several opinions were offered. Most involved the possibility that the significance of the event, followed by the loss of blood, planted an inextricable image of evil in his brain. His thought processes changed. He viewed everything differently than before.

David had become a "Jekyll and Hyde," battling good and evil forces in his own heart. As in most cases, the "evil" was winning.

David Bell refused to deliver another baby. It was as if he feared bringing possible muggers, like the ones who attacked him, into the world. The local medical community was shocked to read in the local newspaper that David had accepted a position with the Women's Health Clinic, the only facility in Roanoke County that performed abortions.

Betty could never forgive him. He had moved out of the house. Twelve months later, the divorce was final.

David, now totally into performing abortions, had begun to develop special instruments to be used in the abortion process. He became a crusader for abortion rights and fought the restrictions against later than second trimester abortions. The small town provided a perfect setting for his experiments.

Alone at night, in his office at the clinic, he would devise the syringe/pump/disposal system that could easily provide an abortion right up until the time of delivery.

David Bell continued to perfect the late term abortion procedure. He had personally designed and created the few simple instruments needed. First, a labor-inducing drug was administered. The baby would then begin its journey through the birth canal as the procedure was ready.

As soon as the top of the baby's head appeared a small incision was made with an exacta type knife. Then a tube was inserted into the skull with the other end connected to a pumping device, which acted to suck the brain from the skull and cleanly deposit it invisibly into a receptacle.

The rest of the baby's body would naturally be birthed within three minutes. It, of course, would be stillborn and disposed of in normal fashion, or preserved for medical experimentation and research, itself a multi-billion dollar industry. He perfected the process and the instruments by performing abortions with patients who had come earlier for the normal first or second trimester abortions. He had convinced them to wait till after their eighth month had begun. The convincing for some was made easier by the payment of $1000 that David would offer them to wait.

The "Bell" method grabbed the attention and interest of abortion providers throughout the country.

Within eighteen months he had written the book on late term abortions and was the recognized leading expert. His books and speaking agenda made it impossible to simply practice medicine. He was also sought after to develop and design clinics that could perform late term abortions.

He demanded, in exchange for his services, and in addition to exorbitant consulting fees, a share of the profits from each clinic he helped get started. David was becoming a very rich man

Chapter 7 Inflight

"You obviously don't know whom you're talking to, young lady!" the woman seated in First Class curtly stated to Janie.

"I am Paula Graves and I will use my cellular telephone whenever I want to. I have many calls to make, so you just toddle on away and mind your own business!"

Janie had just informed her that use of personal cellular telephones was not allowed and that each seat was equipped with an Air Phone from which calls could be made. She did recognize the former Miss America

"I'm really sorry, Mrs. Graves, but regulations prohibit the use of cellular phones in flight. Please, help yourself to the Air Phone," Janie politely suggested.

"First of all, I am not a "Mrs." You can refer to me as Ms. Graves and you are talking to the Vice President of the National Organization of Feminists and I will not be told what and what not to do by some cupie-doll stewardess."

Janie decided that the confrontation had worse possible consequences than any from the actual use of a cellular phone and decided to back away and return to the First Class galley. She silently laughed shortly thereafter though as she watched her passenger try the cellular phone in vain. Flying at this altitude would not provide contact with any cell sites. The Air Phone was the only option So Paula pulled it from its cradle in the seatback ahead and began busily chatting away.

Dr. David Bell heard the entire exchange between the flight attendant and Paula Graves. He had pretended not to listen, and chuckled to himself at the frustration and failure of Ms. Graves to make a connection with her cellular phone. "She obviously doesn't have a satellite phone like mine," he mused.

Bell owned the latest type of phone that relied upon satellite coverage rather than a network of towers. He could communicate from anywhere in the world from any situation. It was based upon similar processes used for Global Position Systems, the latest advance in aviation and marine navigation. The unit would search space for a number of satellites and lock on to signals from the strongest. As a particular satellite's signal weakened from the orbiting, electronically laden craft's movement, it would simply be transferred to another signal from another satellite. The telephone service was expensive, producing monthly bills in excess of two thousand dollars with just moderate use. There was no question that all future wireless communications would come from space, rather than expensively installed and maintained towers.

The technology permitted excellent communication from aircraft as well. However, the governing authorities did not permit the use of satellite or cellular phones on board aircraft.

The Federal Communications Commission (F.C.C.) and the Federal Aviation Administration (F.A.A.) had collaborated to secure legislation prohibiting their use. Safety reasons were cited due to the possible interference with the aircraft's navigational equipment. The flying public accepted the explanation as well, and refrains, as directed by flight crews, from using their cellular and satellite phones in flight.

However, the prohibition of cellular use aboard aircraft was based upon economic, rather than safety, considerations. If interference with the aircraft's navigational ability were the true reason for the restriction, AirPhones, located in the seat backs, could not be used either. They are based upon similar transmission of radio waves, just as cellular and satellite communication.

However, if a passenger could use his own phone onboard a jet, traveling at over five hundred miles-per-hour, it would be impossible to ascertain which cellular sites were being used. The connection would jump from one site to another and therefore make it impossible to track use of the cellular phone for billing purposes. Therefore, the cellular phone companies, licensed by the F.C.C., stood to lose huge sums of money by the free access by passengers.

As an added measure, the newer digital cell phones could use antennae that were more horizontally aimed, rather than the more vertical aspect of the old analog cellular system. That is why digital cellular phones, even if they were legal, will not access a site from an aircraft as easy as the older analog phones would.

"Miss Graves, You're up next."

It was the "gatekeeper," as most Miss America contestants called him. His role was to cue each of the 52 beauties when their performance was near for the talent portion of the pageant.

"I'll be there in a few moments." Paula said without a shred of nervousness.

Paula had always been a natural talent. This prepared monologue on the life of Eleanor Roosevelt was a snap to this multitalented performer. She could play the piano, sing, dance, and act out just about anything. The acting out proved to be her greatest talent...and her greatest liability. Not long into her youth she began to confuse the acting of fiction with the living of reality.

Bob Hansen was a likeable guy. Paula and Bob had several classes together in their senior year at Central High. She had always led him on, even though her thoughts were always on another, usually one who was garnering the most attention at the time. It went from the star football player in the fall to the highest scorer on the basketball team in the winter. In the spring she usually went for pitchers.

"Bob, I've told you before, I'm not going to give you an answer yet."

"But Paula, you're the only one I want to take to the prom!" He was pleading, unlike his normal confidant manner. She had him wrapped up tighter than a drum. He was blinded by her. He couldn't even hear what everyone else, especially the other girls, were saying about Paula.

Descriptive terms like gold digger, egomania, snotty, and too good for everyone, were bandied around about Paula every day. She had no clue until she overheard someone attempt to counsel Bob about his infatuation with her.

"Bob, you've got to get hold of yourself. Paula is a manipulative bitch. She only has herself at heart and she could care less about you or anyone else. No one likes her and she's been this way since elementary school."

It was as if Paula had been hit with a cannonball. Somewhere in her fantasy life she imagined that everyone adored her. She almost buckled when she heard those words. And, they had come from one of the most popular guys in school, one upon whom Paula's attention would land on occasionally.

That night she brooded. She had to show them, show them all one-day how special she was. Her parents were sitting in front of the television that evening while Paula sat alone in her room.

"Come on down, honey," her mother beaconed. "The Miss America Pageant is on."

It was the middle of September and the Louisiana evening had already turned cold. The fire in front of the television set was enough to lure Paula from her room. As she watched the pageant her brain went into high calculation mode. It was there and then that this eighteen year old determined her future.

It started with the local Miss Berkeley County contest. It really was no contest. Paula found out who the judges were going to be and went to work. They were all local businessmen who sponsored the entire event. By the time the Pageant took place she was a shoe-in. She didn't have to go to so much trouble. She was by far the prettiest of the bunch and would have won hands down. It was not like Paula to leave anything to chance, however. It would be the same for the state pageant.

"What is your occupation," asked the registrar for the Miss Louisiana pageant.

"I'm a freshman at Louisiana U." Paula was totally put out by this boring little lady, but she answered politely, nevertheless.

"Well, if you are successful, will you have the time from your studies to represent the state at various functions?"

"Yes, Ma'am," Paula politely replied, chuckling to herself.

Even as Miss Berkeley County for the last eight months, she spent pretty much full time working the system for all it was worth. She was like her own promotion business. She had even learned to generate her own press releases.

She had even arranged to meet the Governor. She had known his reputation for a "player," and especially when it came to ambitious, beautiful young women. She figured that he could make the state title happen. If she was going to be Miss America one day, she would have to become Miss Louisiana first, and she would leave no stone unturned.

"Good evening, Governor." The radar was flowing like a defense silo. The governor was immediately attracted to Paula, not only for her beauty but also for this savvy that she displayed… a savvy that transmitted "I know what I want, and I know what I have to do to get it." Later, at the Regency Hotel, she proved it!

Even Paula was surprised at how easy it was for the Governor to set the whole thing up. Political favors are returned in strange ways. Within hours of being crowned Miss Louisiana she'd already begun plotting the steps to attain her next goal. It was as if she had one thing to prove, that there would be only one possible answer to fictional question that would begin, "...mirror, mirror, on the wall..."

It was dreadfully important for her to become Miss America. As far as she was concerned it was more important than life or death. She didn't know at the time that life and death would be elements in her selfish plan.

. The secret relationship between Paula and the Governor went on for weeks after the State Pageant. Then, it seemed that they both became too busy to carry on this clandestine affair. It was also getting more and more difficult for them to meet. If Paula were going to use her State contacts to catapult her into favorable position in the Miss America contest she would have to get downright inventive.

As always before, give Paula twenty-four hours of a problem and there would inevitably rise an idea in her head that would create shortcuts, end runs, or any device that would cause roadblocks to fall.

The Governor's private phone rang just as he returned from The Annual Prayer Breakfast. This was an annual event that occurred in all states. A National Prayer Breakfast would occur later in the month.

He dutifully attended these annual events and knew all the right buzzwords to use. "Praise the Lord, bless You Brother," He could really pull it off. He could fool anyone; anyone that is, except Paula. They were alike, "Kindred spirits..." they would agree.

"Sorry, Paula, My schedule is packed today."

"Well then cancel something! I really think we should talk, today," Paula replied, "Something has come up that I believe you would consider very important!"

The governor didn't like the tone of her voice. It almost frightened him. He was not used to being put off guard, especially by a woman.

"Okay, okay. Let's meet at the Regency. I'll get a room under the same name as always."

The Governor had no special interest in having sex with Paula this evening. He just determined that the Regency was the only place they could meet without being seen. His Assistant to the Chief of Staff had always been able to secure the room and get the key to the Governor for the late night, back door, rendezvous at the room on the second floor. The assistant had proved his trustworthiness before on several occasions.

"I'm pregnant".

The governor leaned back against the wall and sighed heavily.

"Don't worry," Paula went on, "I'm sure we can get this thing worked out."

"This is beginning to sound like a threat," he thought. Then: "What do you mean 'worked out?'"

"Well, you have your goals, and so do I. You get your cronies and friends to help me win the Miss America Pageant, and I'll keep my mouth shut about this whole thing."

The romance was definitely over now.

"What about the pregnancy?" The Governor needed the right answer now.

Paula was now speaking derisively, "Do you think I'm going to let something like that get in my way. I plan to have an abortion as soon as I can, especially, before I start showing."

The Governor gave assurances that everything he could do, would be done. He knew that the Pageant was run like everything else; it depended on money and sponsors. This would be an expensive maneuver.

"Perhaps, there might be another, less expensive way to handle this," he mused to himself.

A few weeks later, on a dark stretch of a Louisiana highway, Paula was being driven back from an appearance.

"What the…?"

The limo driver had no idea where the truck came from. As he tried to maintain control his mind shifted to the passenger in the back seat. He had to protect Miss Louisiana as best he could. The other vehicle was ramming in from the left side. A deep ravine loomed off the right. There was nothing else that could be done. The driver stared in horror as the limo he was driving made an uncontrolled veer towards the roads edge.

Then, as if in slow motion, the car left the road and headed down the embankment. It came to rest by slamming into a tree. It was silent…for just a few moments. Then Paula, miraculously unhurt in the accident, began to cravingly curse the driver of the truck that had been ramming them. She also began to curse her own driver who she didn't realize was slumped over the steering wheel, dead.

"Are you all right," the ambulance attendant asked.

"Yes, of course I'm all right."

During the hospital examination she had no concern that a pregnancy would be discovered. She was not pregnant. In fact, she had never been pregnant.

Paula never connected the accident with the Governor. He and his friends were able to pull it off, and she would have an inside track on the pageant. It just took money, lots of money, two million dollars to be exact.

She would deny it vehemently, but Bert Parks, in Atlantic City, sang Paula Graves's favorite song in September of 1988. Being crowned Miss America at the age of twenty-two was the icing of a cake that had been baking for most of her life.

As Miss America, Paula dutifully fulfilled all of the appearances that were scheduled. On stage, and at radio and television talk shows, she turned on that effective charm that she utilized so well when it benefited her.

Behind the scenes however, Paula was becoming more and more cynical and callous. Having now attained her lifelong goal, she realized that it didn't fulfill her. It was as if she just never arrived at that place where she could have peace. This frustration played itself out in every relationship and circumstance "off stage."

The term of Miss America lasts just one year and culminates when she crowns the new queen at the next pageant, the following September, in Atlantic City.

Paula dreaded the day and began to loathe the thought of some other young woman taking away the title she fantasized only she should have, ever.

The title-holders from each state assemble in Atlantic City one week before the pageant begins. There, the many dance routines are choreographed, along with the practice stage appearances for each contestant.

97

The outgoing Miss America arrives one day later and takes part in the rehearsals, especially her final walk, and the crowning of her successor.

Paula was staying at a local Holiday Inn, where several members of the National Organization of Feminists were also there making their final plans for the yearly protest of the Miss America Pageant, which they felt was demeaning to women.

Paula had been depressed all week. Three days before the pageant, she met a woman by the ice machine that seemed very friendly. After a short conversation, Paula realized this was a person with a real gift of listening, someone she could tell all her troubles to. The woman happened to be an officer of NOF, and recognized Paula immediately. Some instinct told her to just listen for a while...there may be a golden opportunity here. And there was.

Paula befriended this woman and the others with her. They began to discuss women's rights, at least their views of them. Soon, Paula realized that the feminist movement was the perfect answer because it provided a way she could stay in the spotlight. Besides, there was an angry nature to the whole organization. Paula knew that this was a case of "kindred spirits." The coaching began.

During the Pageant, when she had the microphone for the planned two-minute speech about the year of her reign, Paula Graves stunned the national audience when she proclaimed her new cause.

"Beauty contests are an affront to women everywhere."

She continued, "All women should boycott any company sponsoring any beauty contest. The entire speech took 12 seconds and it was over before the producers knew what hit them. There had been no time to shut off the microphone. She marched off the stage after having dealt the beauty business a blow from which it would never recover.

Some speculated that it was a callous and diabolical act that would ensure that Paula Graves would be the last true Miss America. She had figuratively spray-painted a circled "X" over any following Miss America for years to come.

When Paula Graves walked out of the beauty business she walked into the feminist business. They approached her and treated her like a heroine. She'd found commonality with the leaders of the feminist movement, who had determined she would make an extremely effective public figurehead for the organization, The National Organization of Feminists.

Now a strong and effective voice for abortion rights, Paula was on her way to Anchorage to be one of the featured speakers at the grand opening of Anchorage General's Women's Reproductive Right's Clinic.

Chapter 8   Anchorage

Debbie Cruchon had just finished nailing the poster to the telephone pole three blocks from downtown Anchorage. A woman passerby stopped to read the poster as Debbie stepped a few feet away.

Christian Rally Tonight
When: 7:00 P.M.
Where: Anchorage Center for
            Performing Arts
Speaker: Pastor John Wright
1405 Main St.
Bring Friends
Join us in peaceful protest of the opening of the
Late Term Abortion Clinic at Anchorage Memorial!
Help us stop this horrible sin.

The woman leered at Debbie. "Who do you think you are? Some Christian fanatic who wants to force your belief upon all others?"

"No ma'am," Debbie was stunned by the attack. "We just want to try to stop the killing of babies!"

The woman was now screaming. "You religious bigots, you narrow-minded numbskulls. Who gives you your right to go against a woman's right to choose?"

"A right to choose?" Debbie was gaining her

strength back, still polite. "A right to kill unborn children, right up to just before birth? Do you consider the child?"

The woman was now irate. "It's all about choice, a woman has a constitutional right to terminate her pregnancy!"

Debbie just wanted the woman to think about, and discuss, the baby. She couldn't get the woman to even mention the child.

"Do you think a child is not a person until it's born; that it is an nonliving thing up to the moment of birth?"

The woman wouldn't respond. Her anger and wrath were so prevalent, so mean spirited, that an intelligent conversation would not take place.

"It's a woman's right to choose!"

Debbie tried again, "Look Ma'am, I'm sorry. I don't mean to be trying to persuade you. I understand you are intensely interested in women's rights. Can you also discuss your position as it relates to the unborn child?"

Debbie had often thought that it would be good to have a calm conversation with a pro-abort person. She even reasoned that if a person favored abortion because of an opinion that a fetus is not a living person, there was some understandable logic. She would disagree with it but would better understand why a person might feel that way.

Debbie never found such a person who could

have a reasonable discussion.   There were always the accusations, all referring to Debbie's faith.   There were always heated and unfounded railings about Christians trying to ram their religion down somebody's throat.

The woman appeared to soften momentarily. Then, suddenly her eyes narrowed, and she began yelling.

"You Christians, always trying to get someone to accept your bigoted beliefs!"

Debbie noticed the woman's eyes, how full of hate they were.   It was the same in every confrontation. Debbie remembered a tape she had heard by a minister, John Wright, who was the featured speaker at this evening's rally.

He spoke of his experiences with pro-abort people.   He had determined that they appeared to be driven by an outside force, either by the business aspects of abortion, a multibillion-dollar business, or by something more invisible, maybe spiritual.   Either way, it was well planned and laid out effectively to enlist millions of fervent supporters, some of which may be unknowing.   Their arguments were always extremely emotional, rather than well thought out reasonable explanations.

And then there was the violence.   Abortion clinics were blown up and set on fire.   Abortion doctors were threatened.   Lately there had been a series of horrible crimes where clinic workers had been killed.   These events fueled the ire of pro-abort supporters.

The cause of the Pro-Life movement would suffer greatly with each of these events. Anti- abortion supporters would view these incidents of violence with special abhorrence, not only for the crime itself, and the victims, but also the devastating effect on the peaceful anti-abortion movement.

It was suspected by some that abortion industry representatives might have done the violent acts themselves, because the net result was always favorable to the abortion movement, which made large gains in public sentiment after each violent act.

Historically, criminal investigations would center initially on the person, or organization, that stood to benefit the most from a crime. However, It would have been "politically imprudent" for any police investigator, or district attorney, to even hint at the suggestion this was a "ploy" crime, meant to look as if perpetrated by the opposition.

The woman huffed and walked away. After a few moments, Debbie was able to let her mind return to the task at hand. She drew more comfort realizing that Pastor John was already on his way to Anchorage, aboard Pacific Flight 571.

"Oooh!"

Erica let out a loud groan that passengers, several rows away, could hear. She clutched her protruding belly and leaned forward, almost hitting the stowed tray table on the seat back in front of her.

The pain had come on suddenly like a muscle cramp, but was located exactly where she had been taught from where labor pains would come.

"Oh no," she thought, "I've got to make it till tonight!"

Her thoughts turned into fear, "If I don't get this abortion, he'll kill me!"

It was just a figure of speech. She didn't fear for her life. But, she was terribly afraid of facing him if this child was born. She might be able to go through with the abortion, but she knew that if the child were born, she could never give it up, not after seeing it.

He had convinced her, against her natural instinct, that the fetus is not a living person until it takes its first breath on its own. He was so strong in his persuasion and made her feel stupid if she ever tended to disagree with him.

She loved her boyfriend, or at least thought she did. She feared him as well. Her friends were always trying to get her to break up with him. They recognized the power trip that he held over her.

"Erica, he is no good for you," a friend would say.

"No, you just don't see the part of him I see," Erica replied, defensively.

"Erica, you are blinded by this man. He's ruining your life."

The counsel would never do any good.

Long after the relationship had gone too far she found out he was married. When she began to question whether or not they should keep on seeing each other he succeeded in convincing her they should, and made her feel inferior for even questioning that in this day and age.

"What's wrong with you?" he would demand, rhetorically, "You know I'm the only one who can fulfill you. I'm amazed you don't seem to recognize that!"

"I'm sorry," she cowered, "you're right. You're always right. I know you know best."

Even though he was married she had developed a dependency on him that overruled her judgment. She was weak, and was becoming weaker with every moment she spent with him. In her secret thoughts, she knew that he was bad for her - that he held an unhealthy authority over her. However, she was powerless when it came to him. He even hid the fact that he was a co-pilot with a major airline. He would never allow this relationship to tarnish his selfish goals of running an airline one day.

The deep moan caught Nathan Lambert's attention. He was seated by the window across the aisle, in seat 8F, with no one in the aisle seat. He slid to the aisle seat and leaned across the aisle toward Erica.

"Pardon me, but should I get the flight attendant for you?"

Erica didn't even look up, "No, I'll be alright."

"Oooh, oooh," she moaned again. The pains were continuing, and getting stronger.

She had her eyes closed but was nevertheless jolted by an extremely bright flash, then, another one. She sat upright and opened her eyes.

"What was that?" she was now frightened.

The third flash of the camera almost blinded Erica as she spoke. She was confused initially, but soon realized it was the flash of a camera.

"What are you doing? That frightened me!"

"I'm sorry, but I am a photo-journalist with Lifestyle Magazine and I would really like to take some pictures of you."

"Please, no. I look so terrible and am feeling pretty bad right now. Please ring for the flight attendant."

It was several minutes before Flight Attendant Harold Osteen appeared at her seat.

"What's wrong, Miss?"

"I'm having strong pains in my stomach, I'm sure it's false labor."

She continued, "Could you get me some water?"

Harold immediately supposed that this woman was about to give birth and quickly ran to get Michael. He had completely forgotten the water.

Michael went directly to Erica's row.

"I am going to see if there is a doctor on board,"

"No, I don't need a doctor. Please, can you just give me something to settle my stomach."

Michael had already learned her name from the manifest.

"Erica, I think you are about to have that baby."

Erica motioned for them both to sit down and then explained that she was heading to Anchorage to have an abortion. Harold wanted to keep the matter quiet in order to ensure the abortion would take place. Michael disagreed. He felt that this woman should have medical attention now.

They argued in the aft galley. As always, Harold won. They would do nothing.

It was the fourth flash from the camera that got Janie's attention. Even through the curtain that separates First Class from Coach the flash was clearly seen now that Janie was out of the galley. Once the meals were placed upon the tray tables of her two First Class passengers she decided to investigate the flash from coach. As she walked down the rows she came to the seat occupied by Erica, who, despite a great job of pretending she was fine, was obviously in great discomfort. Janie leaned down.

"Are you alright?"

There was no reply from the young woman, obviously pregnant and in some distress. Janie proceeded to the aft galley and asked Harold and Michael if they were aware of the problem. As Michael started to respond Harold pointed in Michael's face.

"Shut up! Michael sheepishly turned his head at Harold's command.

Janie had no time for discussion. She picked up the PA microphone in the aft galley and was about to call for a doctor when Harold grabbed the microphone out of her hand.

"She does not need a doctor. She is fine!"

Janie could not believe what was taking place. "Listen, I am senior on this flight. Give me that microphone or this will be your last flight!"

She was bluffing. She knew she did not have the authority to cause him to lose his job. Not in this day and age. Homosexuality was protected status in corporate America, especially with the nation's airlines. No matter how egregious the conduct might be, the termination of a homosexual was virtually impossible. Harold momentarily lost sight of that fact and handed the microphone to Janie.

"Is there a physician on board? A passenger is ill."

Dr. David Bell did not want to respond. He had too much on his mind to worry about some airsick passenger.

"Some heroic minded passenger with an EMT certificate was surely on board and would tend to matters," he thought.

Then, "Please, we need a physician to look at a passenger."

And again, "Would a physician please ring the flight attendant call button.

Dr. Bell finally felt too guilty not to respond, primarily because he assumed the flight attendant knew he was a doctor and that the P.A. was probably directed at him anyway. He pressed the call button.

Janie raced to the seat in First Class that had the illuminated call button on its overhead panel.

"Would you kindly look at the passenger in seat 8C?"

Dr. Bell obligingly walked toward coach, not knowing that the ill patient was Erica. It took only one look at her to begin worrying that the birth might actually take place here and now if nothing was done.

"Has your water broken?" he asked.

"No, I don't think so."

Erica started to moan again, and clutch her stomach.

Dr. Bell checked the seat and determined that she was correct in that her water had not broken. However, after timing the pains, he figured it would be any moment. And real labor would follow soon thereafter. If nothing was done soon, the thing he hated most could occur, the birth of a child under his care.

Dr. Bell began to calculate the benefit to his reputation, and to the cause of abortion itself, if he could perform an abortion in flight.

Directly across the aisle from Erica sat Nathan Lambert. He sensed that the young woman across from him was in some sort of discomfort but did not want to inquire as it may take him from his newspaper. He avoided eye contact with the pregnant woman but wondered to himself what kind of story it would be should the pregnant woman give birth in flight.

The thought of photographing and writing the story of a woman giving birth on a flight became more than he could silently bear. He reasoned that pictures of the woman before that baby was born would be just as important to the story as those taken after the baby was born.

Nathan Lambert had grown up in Fresno, California. His journalism interest developed in high school and continued while a student at Cal Berkeley. He had dedicated his life to "the story" and, through pure ambition and determination, had managed to become a popular contributing reporter for Lifestyle Magazine, based in Los Angeles.

With an added talent of photography he was a one-man show. With budget cuts affecting the entire magazine publishing industry, "Lifestyle" could send Nathan anywhere without the additional expense of sending a separate photographer.

Nathan had no inhibition when it came to getting the story. Once the wheels of a story began to roll in his mind all politeness, self-analysis, or patience went right out the window. He was elated when he was chosen for this assignment. Lifestyle Magazine wanted to do an article on the opening of the abortion clinic and there was no-one better then Nathan to create one - to add excitement and intrigue even if the situation was void of them.

The Editor walked into Nathan's office, "Nathan, I've got an assignment for you. Could be a big one."

"Talk to me, what and where?"

"It's the opening of an abortion clinic in Anchorage that will specialize in Late Term Abortions, a real hot topic."

"Yeah, I read about it a few weeks ago on the AP. Is that it?

"Yes, we've booked you on Pacific from here tonight, then out of San Francisco tomorrow. Any problem with that?"

Nathan was single, no family, no ties. "Not at all, I'll be able to get some good coffee, for a change."

The Editor cautioned, "Nathan, I know I don't have to tell you this, but be careful. This late term abortion thing is real hot. Tempers can ... you know!"

"So, what you're saying, is that you don't want another Odessa, right?"

"Exactly!"

Nathan Lambert had been covering the Odessa incident, which involved a religious cult, and its refusal to emerge from their compound on orders from the government's ATF. The cult was thought to have stockpiled weapons.

The standoff ended tragically as fires started, either inadvertently by a government wall-ramming tank, or from within the compound itself. It killed nearly all of the occupants, women and children included. Nathan had been so close to the action that he was wounded in the leg.

He had gotten stuck in crossfire as gunshots rang out from both sides. It was a grazing wound, which made it impossible to determine what kind of bullet caused it. Nathan never knew if the bullet came from the compound or from the ATF. It was accidental, but Lifestyle Magazine did not want to lose their photojournalist.

"Boss, I appreciate your concern. But, you have nothing to worry about. I've learned my lesson, and I have the scar to prove it!"

Janie hurried to the communications panel located by the forward entry door. She rang the cockpit call button.

Damien Pearce answered because Captain Powers had just leaned over to retrieve another chart from his flight kit tucked in a bin just to the left of his seat.

"This is the cockpit."

Janie recognized the voice of Pearce. She didn't like him either and preferred as little dialogue with him as politely possible.

"Let me speak with the captain, please."

"What is it? Tell me and I will tell him."

"Look, I don't have time for this, First Officer Pearce, give me the captain!"

"It's for you, "Damien huffed as he handed the telephone type headset to Captain Powers.

"This is Ross, who is this?"

"Captain, its Janie. We've got a problem."

"Okay, come on up. I'll unlock the door."

The Federal Aviation Administration had ruled decades earlier that cockpit doors would remain locked at all times in flight. Previously, not only were the doors unlocked, they were often times left open, allowing passengers to observe the fascination of all the dials and controls.

However, the era of hijacking that began in the 60's changed all that. Even though the doors were lightweight, and could easily be broken through by a hijacker, the doors would remain locked in flight.

Ross reached back to the rear section of the center control panel and pressed the "door unlock" button. After the click was heard Janie knew the door was unlocked and walked into the cockpit.

"We have a problem with one of our passengers in coach."

She hesitated, gathered her thoughts, and continued.

"She appears to be ready to give birth. I've located a physician."

"Keep me posted, Janie, we're nearing Southeast Alaska and, if it's an emergency, I'll see about landing somewhere close."

"Yes, Sir." Janie said while leaving the cockpit.

Ross reached back and locked the door again.

He was very familiar with southeast Alaska, having spent much of his spare time there fishing and boating. He immediately thought of three airports that would have good hospitals in the vicinity. It was part of a pilot's job to have that type of information in his back pocket. They were 50 minutes from Ketchikan, and 1 hour and 25 from either Sitka or Juneau.

Flight 571 was now cruising at an altitude of 35,000 feet. The route of flight had taken them north of San Francisco, into British Columbia, and then back into US territory over South East Alaska. The flight would pass near Ketchikan,

Juneau, Yakutat, Cordova, then over Alyeska dropping down into the Anchorage area.

Ross was suddenly aware of an air of tension. He looked to his right to see the angry red face of Damien Pearce.

A small contingent had already gathered near Erica's seat, including Dr. Bell, Harold, Michael, and Nathan Lambert. Nathan was continuing his poor acting job as the part of a friend. He had changed film to that of something much faster, which negated the need for a flash.

He was working overtime now getting pictures of all the participants.

Dr. Bell didn't waste any time. He cut right to the issue.

"Erica, you might not be able to wait till Anchorage." He advised.

"But, don't worry, I can perform the abortion right here in flight."

This took everyone by surprise. They had just figured on the excitement of a birth in flight. After a few moments, the thought of an abortion in flight became a very interesting event as well. Perhaps, even more exciting. There began a buzz of enthusiasm, which began to make its way through the aircraft. Word was spreading quickly that an abortion would take place on Pacific Airlines Flight 571.

Abortion was big business. Hundreds of millions of dollars from various sources, mostly taxes, were spent each year for the so-called "constitutional" right of a woman to terminate the pregnancy. Political correctness promised that the dollars would continue to flow unfettered for years to come.

Janie had returned from the cockpit.

"Doctor, if necessary, would you be able to deliver the baby in flight?" Janie was excited at this possibility.

"Miss, you do not have to worry. This young woman had elected to have an abortion later today, in Anchorage." He was almost boasting now.

"I can perform the abortion right here on the airplane."

Janie recoiled with visible shock. Not only at the thought of a medical surgical procedure on board the aircraft. She grimaced at the word "abortion."

Janie and Tom had been married for eight years. They had tried for the last seven to have a child. The tests had come back time and time again with the same result. There was no apparent medical obstacle. Janie could just not get pregnant, and they had agonized over the eventual decision to adopt a child. Janie had decided that, if they could adopt, she would quit her job as a flight attendant, a job she dearly loved.

She was good at it. Her reputation with the airline was flawless. Flight crews enjoyed working with Janie, especially pilots. They knew that the passengers were being pampered, and, that Janie had a real respect for the pilots, and the job they did.

Janie and Tom had finally decided to adopt a child. They had gone through several interviews only to be discouraged time and time again. Few newborns were available, and normally went to younger couples. It was difficult for Janie and Bill to realize that millions of babies were aborted each year while married couples were standing in line to adopt. Janie had just received the disappointing news that they were no longer in the running for a particular newborn child.

There were opportunities to adopt other children, mainly mixed race, or older, from an abusive situation. Janie and Tom considered that for some time until she had a conversation with a friend of a friend who had adopted a sexually abused child.

"Janie, I've got to admit," she said, "If I had it to do all over again I would not do it."

"Why," Janie asked, "I think having any child would be worth it."

"Well, I can only tell you my experiences, and, I've heard of many similar."

"How old is your child now?"

"He's twelve. He was nine when we adopted him."

"What was his background?

"He had come from a foster family. Before that, the State had removed him from a family in which he was sexually molested. We didn't know anything about the molestation thing."

"Didn't the State tell you?"

"No, they are forbidden by law from doing that."

She went on, "Our hearts had really gone out to the boy. It was such an emotional time, not a good time to make a lifelong decision."

"What happened?" Janie asked.

"The first thing that happened is that I got pregnant within three months of the adoption."

"Yeah," Janie offered, "I've heard of that happening quite often."

"Well, " the acquaintance went on, "everything was okay until about six months ago when we discovered that our adopted son was molesting our now three year old daughter."

"What did you do?"

"Our lives are devastated. We've grown to love our son. We don't know what the future holds."

Janie and Tom contemplated these things for some time before deciding not to adopt an older child. They held out for a newborn, even though chances were slim, and growing slimmer.

"What? You can't be serious! Why can't you just deliver the baby?"

Erica appeared to be only partially conscious now. She was not able to respond to Dr. Bell questioning her if she wanted the abortion now. He had decided that performing the abortion during flight would give added credence to the belief that it was a very safe, simple, and clean procedure.

"Miss Page has requested that I perform the abortion right now." He lied.

"I'm going to speak to the captain!"

Janie went directly to the cockpit and knocked loudly, not bothering to ring them on the intercom. Once in, she relayed to the captain what was going on in the cabin.

"Captain, the woman I told you about appears ready to have a baby."

"Well the doctor can deliver it, right?"

"The doctor told me that the woman wants an abortion. She was actually heading to Anchorage to get one. He wants to perform an abortion on this flight!"

Ross was shocked, and then seemed to go into a denial haze. This was entirely too much of a controversy for him. After a few moments he spoke.

"I'm going to try to find someplace to land. We've got to get this thing on the ground!"

He spoke again to Janie, "Janie, get back there and try to keep things calm till we figure out what to do."

Ross's initial response to this situation was to find a suitable place to land. This would absolve him of all responsibility in this conflict. He was against abortion, but this was no place to be a crusader. Let the ground people handle this.

"Damien, get the current weather for Ketchikan, Sitka, and Juneau. Also, check Whitehorse if the weather's bad."

Damien was staring straight ahead, as if in a trance. His face was red and the veins in his neck were puffed up and throbbing.

"Damien," Ross spoke loudly now.

"What, ...uh.... yeah."

Ross changed his mind. "Damien, you monitor Center while I check weather."

In his fifth year as a pilot with Pacific, Damien Pearce did not yet have the seniority to become a captain. He hated being a co-pilot. He wanted to be in command, and felt that he was worthy of command. He had no concept whatsoever of his own weaknesses as a pilot. He blamed others for his troubles in training, complaining to management about the treatment he was receiving.

He had already offended many of the line pilots by requesting to become an instructor in the training department, a position normally reserved for a seasoned captain. He didn't know why the company rejected the idea until one captain he flew with attempted to straighten

Damien out. All this did was solidify his contempt for "those lame brains" that were placed in authority over him.

Most captains preferred not to fly with him. Ross didn't like to fly with him either but did not try to get out of it, as some did. Co-pilots could have a no-fly list by which they could list captains they refused to fly with. Captains did not have such a list for co-pilots. It was ruled that captains should be able to set the mood in the cockpit and ensure it was conducive to safe flight operations, no matter what the personality of the co-pilot was. What Ross disliked most about Damien was the fact that he was compelled by the chemistry of the personality mix to be more authoritative than he wanted to be. Pearce was always challenging that authority, not always verbally - sometimes very subtly - in things that weren't said, as well as things that were.

Damien Pearce was not good at hiding his ambitions. He actually never tried. While in his first year, still on probation with the airline, Damien made a move on the company president's daughter. She was pleasant looking, attractive enough, but she was vulnerable. She had just gone through a bitterly contested divorce and it was well known how wealthy she stood to become through an inheritance one day in the future.

Damien saw her as his opportunity and they were married within six months. Now, four years later, the marriage was a sham. She didn't know it though. Damien hid his exploits well. She was still his ticket. He would run this airline someday. But for now, he was forced to ride shotgun for a bunch of numbskulls that couldn't fly an airplane nearly as well as he thought he himself could.

He was supposed to be off duty today. However, he had found out, from a telephone call with his father-in-law, that this special flight, Pacific Flight 571, was going to happen. He had known about the plans for Air force One, and the special passenger that was supposed to get an abortion in Anchorage. It was necessary for him to ensure that this special someone actually made it to Anchorage. He could have simply gone to Anchorage on a pass, sitting back in First Class and enjoying the ride. No, the cockpit was the only place he could be and not be seen by any of the passengers, one in particular.

Even though married to the airline president's daughter, Damien messed around with other women often. One of these women became pregnant. Normally able to control her Damien was not successful in talking her into having an abortion. However, near the end of the pregnancy she relented and reluctantly agreed to have a Late Term Abortion. She was seated in the cabin and had no idea that the man, who was at the root of all her problems, was seated in the cockpit.

"Ketchikan Flight Service, Pacific 571."

"Pacific 571, Ketchikan, go ahead."

"We need to divert somewhere with medical facilities nearby. Give me the current weather for Ketchikan, Sitka, and Juneau."

"Roger, 571. Current Ketchikan is 600 overcast, visibility 2 and 1/2, winds 100 at 15."

Ross was relieved. The minimums for an ILS approach at Ketchikan were 500 feet ceiling and 3/4 of a mile visibility.

Ketchikan FSS went on: "The glide slope for the ILS 11 is out."

"Oh no," Ross thought, "the glide slope out raises the minimums to 1000 feet and 3 miles." Ketchikan won't do.

"Sitka is reporting below minimums at 300 feet and 1/2 mile visibility. Juneau has also been down all day with 500 feet, visibility 1 mile."

Whitehorse was actually located in Canada. The weather there was normally better than Southeast. It was always a safe haven for aircraft that couldn't land in Southeast and were too low on fuel to head to San Francisco or Anchorage. Today was no exception; the weather at Whitehorse was excellent. "CAVU," ceiling and visibility unlimited.

Ross picked up the microphone. "Vancouver Center," we have a medical emergency on board and must divert to Whitehorse."

As he spoke the words Ross breathed a sigh of relief at the thought of this problem soon to be over.

"Roger, sir, but Whitehorse has no medical facilities. We can give you a heading if you like, however. Please advise."

One additional thing the controller wanted to know, "Also please state the nature of the medical emergency."

After a thirty-second delay, "Okay Center, we'll continue to Anchorage," said Ross, "Also, the medical situation involves a pregnant passenger."

That seemed to be all the information ATC wanted.

Everything had happened so fast that Ross Powers was increasingly grasping the weight of the situation. He had always been against the liberal abortion policies but had never gotten involved in the debate. The issue had never touched him personally and he was able, therefore, to keep from being identified one way or other in the issue. This was different. He was in command of this aircraft and thereby responsible for everything that took place. An abortion would not be performed on this aircraft without the concurrence of the captain.

Damien finally spoke. "You are not planning on standing in the way of this, are you?"

Ross ignored Pearce's question. He thought for a few moments...seemed like hours, then reached up to the overhead panel and rang the Flight Attendant Call button.

"This is Janie."

"Janie, I need to speak with that physician. Send him up here."

Allowing any non-approved person into the cockpit was a violation of Federal Aviation Regulations. However, under emergency authority, the captain could deviate from regulations. This was an emergency and Ross knew there was nothing in the procedure manual that covered this type of situation.

"Captain, my name is Dr. David Bell. I am a board certified obstetrician and I have examined the young woman."

Dr. Bell continued as if he were lecturing at a medical conference.

"She is likely to give birth within the next hour or so and she has requested an abortion. I plan to perform it on this aircraft."

Ross was struck by the matter-of-fact way the person before him was discussing an abortion. He was also somewhat inflamed by the arrogance of this doctor to state what was or was not going to happen on this aircraft. Before he had a chance to respond, Damien piped in:

"Doctor, do whatever you need to do, we have medical kits on this airplane, and..."

Ross interrupted Pearce in mid sentence.

"Wait just one second here, gentleman. I am in command of this aircraft and I will decide whether or not a surgical procedure is undertaken!"

Ross's confrontational attitude surprised even himself.

Dr. Bell stated, "Captain, it is my medical opinion that the procedure can and should be performed on this flight."

Dr. Bell continued in a now threatening tone, "Any attempt on your part to stop it is wrong. It is her Constitutional right to have an abortion, on this plane or anywhere else."

The physician was gone from the cockpit before the captain could respond. Captain Ross Powers was faced with the greatest challenge of his life, and he only had a minute or two to decide on a course of action. It would have been infinitely better, he thought, if he could have just had several hours to mull over the direction he should pursue. No such luxury was here at this moment, when he needed it most.

After a few moments, he made the decision. There will be hell to pay, but sometimes it can't be helped. He knew what he must do.

He again rang the Flight Attendant Call button. Janie answered. Ross spoke.

"Janie, the flight paperwork advised me of the presence of an armed Federal Marshall in coach. Find him and send him up here immediately."

It was not unusual for armed law enforcement personnel to be aboard commercial airliners. In fact it was practically an everyday event, especially, to and from Alaska. It was also normal for government representatives to be armed, even when they weren't escorting prisoners. Ross had at one time objected to armed persons on board. He especially had trouble understanding why Postal Inspectors would always be armed.

One-day a flight attendant's curiosity about armed individuals reached the limit. The airplane was still at the gate, and she appeared at the cockpit door.

"Captain, I just don't understand why all these law enforcement people must be armed while riding as passengers."

"I don't know either," he stated while looking around, ". Perhaps it's a testosterone thing!"

"No sir, I assure you it's not!" The voice was not recognizable. And, it was stern, yet respectable. It was an armed policeman preparing to go to his seat as he overheard the comments while passing by the cockpit door.

"I carry my weapon for one reason. That is the only way I always know where it is. It would kill me to learn that my weapon, out of my possession, became used in the killing of some innocent child."

The point made its target. "Thank you, Officer," Ross was conciliatory, "after all these years I think I now understand."

Janie checked the manifest and determined the name of the marshal, and which seat he was occupying, 21A. Frank Grafton was going to Anchorage to pick up a prisoner and escort him back to San Francisco.

"Yes, I'm the federal marshal," he went on, "my name is Frank Grafton."

Moments later, a large black man dressed in a dark suit appeared at the cockpit door. Janie knocked and the door was immediately opened from within. They entered, the marshal ducking his head so his 6'5" frame could fit through the door.

In coach, Dr. David Bell had become almost a madman. Deep down he was so conflicted that, in order to continue his path, he would nullify any doubts that would creep into his conscience. He had lost all logic, logic that might have brought him to question why he just didn't let the girl have the child. This one young woman's failure to have an abortion couldn't be that important. He didn't even consider that a botched abortion, in a non-sterile environment, might have a negative impact on the cause.

To David Bell, however, this abortion was dreadfully important. He could feel it, he was driven; and didn't know by whom.

"Captain, my name is Frank Grafton. I'm a Federal Marshall."

Frank Grafton started his law enforcement career as a small town beat policeman. After 5 years his lifelong dream of being an F.B.I. agent was finally realized. After 6 months at the Academy in Quantico, Virginia, this young agent dedicated himself to being the best. He worked and studied hard, and, was recognized and rewarded with interesting assignments.

One such assignment was a kidnapping case involving the 15-year-old daughter of a wealthy and highly connected General Contractor. The case was attracting national interest and had cast young Frank Grafton into the spotlight. It couldn't have ended better. Thanks to the efforts of Frank, the young girl was returned to her parents unharmed, after two weeks on the case.

Frank was not at all interested in the fame that followed. He refused interviews that would continue to catapult him into the national spotlight. After a while, the interest abated and Frank hoped to return to normal F.B.I. assignments. However, the F.B.I. wanted to capitalize on the reputation of Frank, which enhanced the Bureau's own image.

Frank Grafton was assigned as an investigator in the TAT Flight 465 incident, a 747 departing New York's JFK International Airport that mysteriously exploded and fell into Long Island Sound. He would report directly to the Investigator in Charge.

Frank jumped into the investigation with both feet. Within days, however, he began to be frustrated in his efforts by invisible lids that were being placed on the active investigation. He was not allowed to interview representatives of the airline, or the airplane manufacturer. He soon realized that his roll was that of a reflector device, to reflect negative press directed to the Bureau, who had taken total control of the investigation.

The National Transportation Safety Board, NTSB, historically had control of civilian aircraft accidents. For several days, even the NTSB was locked out. There was something peculiar about this investigation and Frank was beginning to wonder why.

He began to conduct a little investigation on his own. He secretly met with pilots, safety representatives from the airlines, and witnesses, many of who said that they had witnessed a streaking object heading straight for the ill-fated aircraft just moments before the explosion.

Word of Frank's independent activity made its way to the White House itself, who had placed fake witnesses to act as spies in order to detect any eager and crafty investigative work, usually by an investigative reporter from any of several national newspapers.

The hammer fell in a sudden and forceful moment. Frank Grafton was summarily removed from the investigation and immediately assigned to Lompoc Federal Prison, as a prisoner escort. His previously promising career had just plummeted to the lowest rung of the ladder.

"Frank, there is a problem developing in coach and I need your help."

Ross explained the situation to date. He stated that the abortion was not to take place on this aircraft and that it was Frank's job to keep everyone away from the passenger, now known to be Erica Page in seat 8C.

"I will instruct you further as things develop. In the mean time take up a position with the woman and keep me posted through Janie."

With an affirmative nod and a simple "Yes Sir," Marshall Frank Grafton departed the cockpit while at the same time drawing his weapon from the holster.

Captain Ross Powers was now committed. He had elected a course of action and there was no turning back. Not now. He hadn't noticed the look of astonishment on his co-pilot's face.

Amidst a great deal of commotion throughout the entire aircraft Nathan Lambert's camera was preserving each detail. He was witnessing an event that had all the intrigue of a small-scale war

Gathered around Erica were the Doctor, and both Michael and Harold, who had now jumped into the scene to assist the doctor with whatever he needed. Suddenly, Frank Grafton appeared. A 38-caliber pistol was in his hand and pointed in the general direction of the group huddled around Erica.

"Listen up, I am Federal Marshall Frank Grafton. I have been instructed by the captain to prevent an abortion from being performed. Now, all of you move away from the girl!"

As everyone moved away Frank was shocked to see this woman so far along in her pregnancy. He moved to the seat next to her, placed one knee on the seat so as to be in a position to see all around him, and began the vigil of keeping everyone from touching her.

Dr. Bell was incredulous, and went directly to the aft lavatory where he could not be seen. He pulled his satellite phone from his coat pocket, and began dialing. He pressed the #1 speed-dial button.

Chapter 9   Los Angeles, CA

Professor Tallmadge normally received calls through the switchboard of California University Law School. Only two persons had the number of his cellular phone. One was the President of The United States; the other was Dr. David Bell.

When the phone rang, Professor Tallmadge was in the middle of a lecture, which included excerpts of his arguments in the "Lincoln" case. He looked at the Caller ID screen and saw only that it was a call from a satellite network. He immediately excused himself from the class to go into the hallway to answer the call. It was initially a small disappointment that it wasn't the President calling, but he was always happy to hear from Dr. David Bell.

"Ron, fate has dealt us a magnificent opportunity." He continued on describing the events to date on Flight 571.

"I need for you to bring whatever power-to-bear you can muster up to force this lunatic captain out of the way. This abortion could go a long way in proving the ease and safety of the LTA. There are still some idiots that need to be convinced."

Somewhere in the rushed conversation, and, in the midst of some static, the word "armed" came through.

"I will contact the President immediately."

The conversation was over in less than 4 minutes. Professor Tallmadge did not return to his class. There was an important call to a Washington D.C. number that had to be made.

Tallmadge taught Constitutional Law at California University School of Law in Los Angeles and had for many years been the leading legal advisor to the United Civil Liberties Union, UCLU. He was known as one of the nation's top legal minds, and had argued many cases before the U.S. Supreme Court, the most famous being the recent "Lincoln" decision, which eliminated restrictions on when abortions could take place.

The earlier limitations had provided the availability of abortion up to the end of the first trimester. Then, political pressure prompted the increase to the end of the second trimester. The "Lincoln" decision, argued before the Supreme Court by Ron Tallmadge himself, allowed abortions to take place all the way up to the moment the forehead of the baby was visible.

While in Washington to appear before the Supreme Court, Professor Tallmadge stayed at the White House, ironically, in the Lincoln Bedroom. He was a frequent guest. His friendship with President Jenson had grown since he was first summoned to advise The President regarding constitutional legal matters. It was no secret to any in the legal community that Ron Tallmadge would most likely be the next U.S. Supreme Court Justice.

His monumental climb up the legal ladder to national prominence was unlike any other. When he was less than five years out of law school he represented two gay men who had been ejected from the dance floor at a county fair. The successful outcome of that trial cast his niche and identity for liberal causes. It was inevitable that Ron Tallmadge would take up the legal cause for abortion. He began to represent abortion clinics.

In the mid 80's, Operation Rescue, a national organization dedicated to non-violent blockades of abortion clinics, had orchestrated hundreds of abortion protests. At a predetermined time and place carloads of anti-abortion activists would arrive for final dispatch to the site of the protest.

Only the leaders would know which clinic would be targeted that morning and soon hundreds of carloads of people, many of whom had never demonstrated for anything before, would be following lead cars to an unsuspecting abortion clinic. The other side, the pro-abortion activists, ultimately learned how to infiltrate the ranks by pretending to be pro-lifers.

A contingent of hundreds of pro-choicers would be standing by for last minute determination of the targeted clinic. In many cases, the pro-choice activists would arrive at the clinic even before the pro-lifers.

These protests always resulted in criminal charges being filed against the pro-lifers. Professor Tallmadge would represent the clinics in ensuring that the local District Attorney adequately prosecuted the anti-abortion protesters. Along with his duties of teaching Constitutional Law, he was a very busy man. His retainers by the owners of abortion clinics were rapidly making him a wealthy man as well.

Tallmadge always kept his miniature cellular phone charged up and in his pocket. With a potential Supreme Court justice position in the future, he would never want to miss a phone call from The President. Nor would he want to miss a call from Dr. David Bell, from whom he had already amassed a small fortune.

Professor Ron Tallmadge had been of enormous assistance to James Jenson during the initial bid for the presidency. Once in office, the President continued to rely on Tallmadge's keen and scholarly insight to the volatile issue of abortion. It was President Jenson who first suggested Ron Tallmadge for the role of arguing "Lincoln" before the Supreme Court. It really didn't matter who actually argued the case. The outcome had been pre-determined. However, much national prominence would naturally flow to the one selected.

Tallmadge telephoned the White House. His call was immediately transferred to Air Force One.

"Mr. President, I just received a call from Dr. David Bell who is aboard a flight from San Francisco to Anchorage. He's on his way to be part of the opening ceremonies of the clinic at Anchorage General."

"Yes, Ron, I have been staying well abreast of the opening of the clinic. We are all excited about it."

"Mr. President, I have an extremely urgent situation to discuss."

"What is it, Ron?"

"Sir, there is a woman that's accompanying him."

"Yes, that's right, Paula Graves of NOF."

"Not her, sir, this involves the young woman that's traveling with them to Anchorage to receive the first LTA."

"What about her?"

"Apparently, she has gone into labor on the flight. Dr. Bell wishes to perform the abortion in flight. The captain is prohibiting it."

"Ron, I don't really give a rip about the girl. What urgent issues does this involve?"

"Well, the way I see it, it is a jurisdictional issue."

"Go on, explain," replied the President.

Well sir, we've made great strides to eliminate a State's jurisdiction to in any way limit total and unfettered access to abortions."

He President replied, "Yes, thanks to my appointments to the Court."

Continuing, "So, how does this affect that jet? Is it a big deal just to let the damn woman have the kid?"

The Professor continued, "The 'big deal' is that suddenly we're allowing someone else, in this case, an airline captain, to have jurisdiction over whether or not an abortion can take place."

"Go on," The President was listening intently.

"Mr. President, I can't overstate the legal significance of this event."

The seriousness of that statement from such a respected legal mind secured the President's interest.

"This dilemma is a grave one. It could bring up issues that could impede the legal progress we've been making, and actually undo some gains in the unrestricted access to abortions."

"Are you saying that one airline captain's refusal to allow in in-flight abortion could impact the entire pro-choice movement.

"Absolutely! The success of the pro-choice movement is directly tied to the inability of any person, entity, or government, to restrict any woman's right to an abortion."

"So, relate that to the aircraft situation."

"This airline captain is licensed by the Federal Aviation Administration. He derives his command authority from a body of law contained in the F.A.R.s, the Federal Aviation Regulations."

"Go on, I'm beginning to see where you're going."

"Since the F.A.R.'s give him his command authority, and, if he uses that authorized authority to restrict access to an abortion, it is tantamount to the United States Government sanctioning his actions."

"Ron, you're brilliant. I would have never made that connection."

"Thank you, Mr. President, there's more."

"Continue, I'm making notes."

"In my studies of history I have always noted that military successes were often tied to the genius of leaders in not underestimating the capabilities of the enemy. Sir, this is war. Our primary enemy is the increasingly well-organized pro-life movement. They have obtained the services, mostly volunteered, of some of the best legal minds of the country. They will have a field day with this for the reasons I've previously stated."

"Now I see how they could take one incident aboard a commercial flight and turn it into a legal fiasco," the President mused.

"Exactly! At the least, they would tie up the courts with this complicated legal question. Conservative judges might agree to curtail abortions till this was finally settled."

Ron Tallmadge completed his dissertation with a remark that jolted the President: "And Sir, the courts could tie this thing up well beyond the next election. If this debacle is allowed to happen on your watch, it could greatly affect your chances of being reelected."

The President almost dropped the phone. Tallmadge cleverly remained quiet so his last statement could have its full impact. Mrs. Jenson, who had only heard one-half of the conversation, curious at how intently the President had been listening, saw the color leave his face.

Then, "Ron, I could have never imagined such massive fallout from the actions of one small, insignificant, individual.

"Mr. President. It's called the 'Butterfly Effect'."

"The what?"

"The Butterfly Effect. It's a scientific theory named from the effect of the waving of a butterfly's wings."

"Explain."

"There's a theory that if a butterfly waves its wings in, say, Asia, it sets off a minute turbulence that ultimately impacts weather phenomena around the entire world, including hurricanes, tornadoes, monsoons, etc."

"So, huge consequences can be produced by seemingly inconsequential events."

"Exactly, Mr. President."

"Then, this airline captain, our little 'butterfly', is about to have his wings clipped!"

This would be the second major crisis for the young president. His first term had gone off without a hitch. However, here in the middle of his second term this second national issue threatened to dismantle his agenda. Once his lifelong goal to be elected president had been fulfilled James Jenson was feverishly determined to leave a legacy. He wanted to be known as a great president - even the greatest president - and it didn't matter to him how it was accomplished.

It was interesting that this second crisis involved aviation, as did his first. The cover-up of the greatest and most costly mistake ever made had called upon every deceptive and diabolical fiber of his mind. It had also required the calling in of all favors. After all, this mistake had been made by the greatest military machine in the history of mankind, and that of the leader of the free world.

How that super secret anti-missile missile could miss its target during that highly organized test is anybody's guess. What is no guess is the damage and loss of life it caused when it calculated a new target once the intended one had been missed. There was nothing anyone could do to stop the missile from honing in on the number three engine of the 747 - not all the generals of the military – and, tragically, not any of the two-hundred and eighty unsuspecting passengers who had been aboard.

The test had been so secret that only those with the highest security clearances were allowed knowledge and participation. The disbelief that initially followed the destruction of the airliner paved the way for the greatest cover-up in history.

It was necessary for national security. There would have been pandemonium, if not revolution, had the public discovered that their own military had been responsible.

It was the president who had made the decision. Another explanation for the explosion would have to be created. The cause would ultimately be laid at the feet of the manufacturer. But, if they didn't squawk, the president would see to it that hundreds of billions of dollars worth of aircraft orders would come from most of the nation's airlines. After all, there had been favors, and it was payback time. In fact, the manufacturer was allowed to absorb a competing aircraft manufacturer without one peep from the Anti-trust lawyers.

He had convinced the military leaders that it was a matter of national security. They balked at first, and then assented. Once the door of truth had been closed, it could never be opened again. There would eventually be ruined lives, emotional and mental breakdowns, even suicides. There was only one who would not suffer. President Jenson had staved off the biggest threat to his legacy agenda.

And now he would handle this crisis with the same cool. James Jenson didn't care one way or the other about abortion. He only cared that his mantle of greatness was attached to this issue. He would rise to the occasion. The enemy was now on domestic soil and these anti-abortionists would not succeed - not for a moment - not on his watch.

James Jenson's political life had begun in high school. His popularity had earned him the suggestion by some to run for his Freshman Class Presidency. The gratification he experienced by being elected was more hallucinogenic than any drug could ever be. It provided a motivation for academic excellence - a focus. It determined who he was.

At a young age he learned that political ramifications shaped his position on a particular issue. It took over his thought processes, his relationships, his worldview. It was his religion. His view of God was even shaped by the politics of the day. In his youth, God was an acceptable reality in politics. As he grew older and aspired to higher office he leaned to more humanistic viewpoints that became more politically expedient.

James Jenson's rise to the highest office in the nation was tied to abortion. He had recognized that this was the defining issue that could bring him national acclaim as well as the necessary funds for the campaigns.

Abortion money was big - and there were myriads of ways this money could be channeled to a Presidential campaign. Millions of dollars could be donated from one source through the orchestrated individual donations of millions of militant abortion rights activists.

James Jenson's champion cause was the LTA. In one term of office he had been able to replace two retiring Supreme Court Justices. He was virtually guaranteed of another two if he was reelected to a second term. Though the election was still a year away the reelection campaign had been going on since first taking office.

"Get me the Secretary of Transportation, the FAA Administrator, and the Chairman of the Joint Chiefs."

Except for Secretary of Transportation Miller, none of the others had been previously summoned by the President, himself. After a twenty-five minute conference call each appointee knew what actions were expected of them. Every resource within air transportation, the US Military, and the State of Alaska would be brought to bear to insure that the abortion on Flight 571 would not be prevented.

Transportation Secretary Robert Miller had previously known what it was like to receive an urgent call from the President. The first had been related to the TAT 700 tragedy off the coast of Maine. His subsequent call to F.A.A. Administrator Noel Howard was taken by surprise. Noel Howard had formerly been an airline pilot before being appointed to a high position within the F.A.A. His ardent and financial support of President Jenson had resulted in his being elevated to Administrator once the President took office.

James Jenson was by far the most effective administrator in the history of the United States Presidency. He had appointed persons to important posts who would do anything the President demanded. They were smart men, but totally and unabashedly dedicated to James Jenson. One word from the President and it was like a pack of pit bulls being set loose for a particular task. No further involvement of the President was necessary.

There was no time to lose. In spite of the hour each of the men went to their respective offices and began to bring the world down on Ross Powers, the captain of

Pacific Flight 571.

Communications aboard airliners include a device called "SelCall", or selective call. This allows the jet to be contacted from someone on the ground. The primary purpose was for the airline to be able to contact the crew of the aircraft without having to relay information through Air Traffic Control.

The chimes of the Selcall always take pilots by surprise. They are so seldom used that the chime silencing buttons are usually difficult to locate. The bells are loud. There had been an old airline story about an all-night cargo flight from New York to Los Angeles. The pilots had been flying all night after no sleep the day before and had all fallen asleep. The autopilot flew them at their cruise altitude of 35,000 feet. In spite of several attempts of ATC to call them on the radio, the two pilots had gone in such a deep sleep that they couldn't hear the radio and had over-flown LAX. They were headed out over a dark black ocean at 35,000 feet.

Finally the SelCall chimes went off and both pilots were jolted from their slumber. All they could see was dark ocean below. Fortunately, they were only thirty miles west of LAX by that time, and a descent and landing were accomplished without further difficulty. It was, however, the last flight ever flown by either of the two pilots.

Both Ross and Damien jumped when the chimes went off. Once they were silenced the company frequency was dialed into the #2 radio.

"This is 571, go ahead."

"571, this is Chief Pilot Ward, let me speak with Captain Powers."

Ross was encouraged at the thought that his boss was on the radio. Surely, total support would come from his old friend. They had started the airline together as classmates. When Rusty and his wife were having marital difficulties it was Ross and Mary who counseled them and took them to church. The marriage had been saved. Now, during the most bizarre crises of Ross's life, his boss - and his friend - was there for him.

"Surely, he will support my decisions," he thought.

"Ross, this is Rusty. All hell is breaking loose down here on the ground over that abortion. I can tell you this. Let the abortion take place or risk incredible consequences!"

Ross couldn't believe his ears. "Rusty, are you ordering me to allow the abortion. I can't let it take place - not under my command."

"Ross, you have no choice. The airline, F.A.A., even the White House is involved in this. Let the abortion take place."

Ross thought for what seemed like an hour before responding. It was only 15 seconds." I'm sorry, Rusty. This is still my call. I can't do it."

"Ross, I hate to do this - you are hereby relieved of command of that aircraft. Your first officer is to take command right now."

Ross couldn't believe his ears. Never before, in all aviation history, had an attempt been made to terminate command in flight. It couldn't be done. Furthermore, the first officer did not even possess the necessary type rating, an add-on to an Air Transport Pilot License, which allows the holder to fly command. The whole idea was bizarre. Ross rejected it.

"Rusty, there is no way, legal or otherwise. I am in command and will stay in command as long as we're in the air!"

Damien had been listening. He couldn't believe that his fantasy was coming true. At last he would be in command. Even though he did not have the proper credentials to command the 737 he had now received full authority.

In order to fly captain in the airlines one had to receive a special "type rating" in the aircraft. This training would only take place when the pilot was senior enough to obtain a captain's bid. Weeks of additional training would also take place before a pilot was released by training to fly "in command" of a flight.

Damien had neither the training nor the type rating. He was, of course, perfectly able to take command of the aircraft in the event of captain incapacitation, but this was different. This was authorized mutiny.

Ross and Damien sat silence for just a moment before Damien commanded:

"Powers, I am now in command of this flight."

The words had rolled effortlessly off Damien's lips as if they had been practiced several times before. In fact, they had.

Ross took one large breath before responding.

"Pearce, you listen up - and listen up good!" Ross was firmly in control.

"You are not in command of this flight," Ross declared, "No-one can authorize you for this and I am continuing to be the captain whether you like it or not!"

As Damien picked up his microphone to inform the Chief Pilot, Ross reached down and twirled the frequency selector off of company frequency. Damien grabbed Ross's hand and tried to move it off the dial. That was a mistake.

The situation in the cockpit had now deteriorated into a physical confrontation. The defining outcome, however, was controlled by the immense physical differences between Ross and Damien. Damien was 5'6" tall and weighed 145 pounds. Ross was 6'2" tall and weighed 205 pounds. Ross worked out, Damien did not.

When Ross took hold of Damien's hand the pain was more than Damien had ever experienced. Three of Damien's fingers made cracking sounds as they fractured. Years of pent up dislike of this arrogant jerk were now focused on the three middle fingers of Damien's hand. If Janie had not just walked into the cockpit and yelled, Ross may have broken Damien's arm.

"Captain, what are you doing," She asked.

Ross, stunned by his own actions, immediately released the grip, and sat back in his seat. For a few moments, he stared straight ahead as one does during the collection of thoughts. Except for the moaning coming from the co-pilot's seat no other sound was made for a complete minute. Ross knew that he was commanding his last flight ever. The die had been cast. This stand would surely cost him his career. He didn't realize that it could cost him much more.

Back in Coach, Nathan Lambert's camera was clicking away. In spite of Sky Marshall Frank Grafton's protest, Nathan knew that there was no way the camera could be grabbed by Grafton without losing his guarding position near Erica.

"Grafton, this call is for you. It's the President of the United States."

Dr. Bell's call to Ron Tallmadge had resulted in this highly unusual communication.

Dr. Bell handed his satellite phone to Frank.

Frank was very suspicious. "Yes?"

This was a strange flight and bizarre things were happening.

"Maybe it was the President." Frank just listened.

"Marshall Grafton, this is President James Jenson. The captain on your flight has just been relieved of his command. The first officer is now in charge. I order you to not interfere with the abortion that Dr. Bell is to perform. Do you understand?"

Frank initially did not know how to respond. He was not a Jenson fan, yet this was his boss of bosses. He did recognize the voice, and after a few seconds, did not question that it was, in fact, the President.

"Yes sir, loud and clear," Frank replied.

"Now, it's important you don't blow this, Marshal. We're counting on you to come through for us on this."

Frank thought back to the past, and how his career was ruined because of one man.

"Absolutely, sir. I understand completely now."

When Dr. Bell heard Frank's reply he deduced that the opposition had been eliminated and that the abortion could take place. He had been standing there with his attaché case at the ready and now was moving directly toward Erica.

It didn't take Frank one moment to react. He pointed the pistol at the doctor. "One more move, Doctor, and it will be your last."

Looking down the barrel of that pistol sent David Bell back in time to that fast-food rest room in Sacramento. He reacted so abruptly that his brief case fell to the aisle floor and opened, spilling the contents.

There on the floor was the apparatus he had planned to use. There was going to be no sterilization - didn't need to be - the only flesh this instrument was going to come in contact with was the head of the fetus, if you can call it a fetus when it's coming down the birth canal. "Fetus" is an easier thing to terminate than a "baby!"

There was also another item tucked into the briefcase that no one saw – a small 38-caliber pistol that Dr. Bell carried for protection. He was too afraid to use it now. He was familiar enough with airplanes to know that a gun battle at 31,000 feet would have disastrous consequences.

Frank had ordered all but Janie away from Erica. Janie had already informed Frank, and the captain, that she was perfectly capable of delivering the baby if needed. She was a former nurse, and still active as a 1st Lieutenant in the Air Force Reserves as a MedEvac nurse. On weekends she would participate in reserve drills aboard the military C141 out of McCord AFB. This was another job she would gladly give up if she could adopt a child.

Her previous calls for a physician were standard procedure in a passenger illness event. She had been quite confident that, if no-one responded, she could have handled the situation entirely by herself. She had now developed unspoken thoughts that, if the possibility of adoption fell through, perhaps Erica would give this baby up.

That is, she thought, "if the baby were able to survive the attempts on his or her life," she reasoned.

"Erica, let us move you to First Class. You will be much more comfortable."

Janie had suggested this after determining with Frank that it would be easier to watch over her there. Erica was still too dazed to respond. Frank picked her up, gently, after temporarily holstering his pistol. With Janie leading the way he carried her forward, through the First Class curtain, and into the most forward First Class seat.

He drew his pistol from the holster again and immediately ordered Dr. Bell and Paula Graves into coach.

"Now, listen to me," Paula Graves began. "Put that gun down immediately or I'll make sure your life becomes a living hell!

"Ma'am, I'm sure you've made many men's lives a living hell. For now, perhaps you should consider your own life."

The gun made a clicking sound, as if being cocked. Frank was bluffing, but Paula Graves didn't know that. The sound of the click was enough to make this belligerent woman tremble. She left First Class.

Draper Powers had been sitting near the aft cabin, staring out the window, and listening to his Ipod. He hadn't noticed the commotion going on further up front but was now sensing that something was wrong.

Draper was the third of four children. He had been a pure delight to raise. Ross and Mary would often say that Draper was never taught to say "please" and "thank you." He just simply said those things, naturally, since he began to speak. He loved his dad, and, like all the kids, enjoyed flying on "Daddy's jet" as often as he could.

Flight 571 was Draper's turn. Next flight would be Joy's turn, then Faith, then Price. Mom would jump in occasionally as well, which always resulted in an evening of dinner and romance for Ross and Mary - even after twenty-six years of marriage.

Draper's love for his father was made abundantly clear to his dad one day. Ross and Draper were riding up a chair lift together at Crystal Mountain Ski Area, on a beautiful sunny day in late March when spring skiing conditions were prevalent. Draper and Ross loved to ski together. Actually, Draper snowboarded while Dad skied. During one of the chair rides the father and son were discussing how beautiful the scenery was.

It was enough that Ross even remarked, "Thank you, Lord."

The discussion turned, as lightly as is possible, to religious things, and centered on the subject of prayer. Ross had brought the subject up because he had listened to a Christian radio program on the way up to the mountain earlier that morning.

Draper had been asleep in the van most of the way up. Ross's heart had been touched by the subject matter of the program and was being somewhat reflective about how often his thoughts were about God. It was man-to-man, not heavy - actually, it was a light, but sweet, conversation between father and son.

Draper offered that there were times when he thought of God - and, prayed to God. He said that those times most often coincided with a desire for something. So he would pray for that something. The next thing he would say would mean more than riches to his dad.

"I pray when I ski with you, Dad."

"What do you mean?"

"When we go skiing, and I lose sight of you, I always pray that you won't get hurt. The last time Price was with us we stopped and looked back for you, but couldn't see you." He went on, " I said that I hate it when I can't see Dad. Price said that he hated it too."

Draper did not know what that meant to his dad. For the rest of the day, Ross could ponder little else than the knowledge that his son, both his sons, loved him very much.

Draper seated in 18A, placed the earphones on the seat beside him. He started to walk forward before Harold stopped him.

"Draper, I suggest you just sit still. Your father is in deep trouble and you just stay out of the way."

That was all that Draper needed. He brushed Michael's arm aside and quickly walked forward. He couldn't believe his eyes when he saw a man holding a gun in plain view.

"Oh no, a hijacking," he thinks.

All he knew was that he had to get to his dad. He figured that if he appeared not to see anything the hijacker would just let him pass. He figured right. The man with the gun paid him no mind at all as Draper passed Erica's seat and proceeded further forward to the cockpit door. Draper had never been in the cockpit during flight - it was against Federal Aviation Regulations for non-approved persons to be there in flight. But this was different - there was a hijacking going on.

He knocked. The door opened. Draper went right into his dad's outstretched arms. Though still seated in the left pilot chair, Ross twisted toward the rear and embraced his son.

"Dad, what's going on? Are we being hijacked?"

"No, Son, the man with the gun is a Federal Marshall. He is doing what I've instructed him to do."

Draper looked over at Damien, who was still bent over in pain.

"What's wrong with him?" He asks.

"Son, I'll have to explain later. Right now, I want you to sit behind me in the jumpseat, here."

Ross knew that this was against all rules. But rules had gone out the window. All he wanted to do was get this airplane to Anchorage, as soon as possible. He had already increased the cruise speed by selecting the maximum mach speed the 737-800 could fly at that weight. There was ample fuel on board to cover the additional burn at the higher speed.

The news services were already buzzing with excitement. Some of the passengers' Airphone calls had alerted them with the situation. By the time the aircraft was two hours out from Anchorage, CNN had conducted Air Phone interviews with several passengers. The networks were frantic to gain more information and were talking to anyone they could.

Ross had been unaware of the Air Phone communication going on until receiving an intercom call from Janie. Ross immediately pulled the circuit breaker for the Air Phone and the communication by passengers to those on the ground were terminated. It was good that he had done that for, unknown to him, the frantic responses on the ground to what was happening aboard Flight 571 were so distorted that some passengers had been told that the flight was in the control of an insane and dangerous captain.

Many, who had previously been caught up in the abortion issue, now feared for their own safety. And the man with the gun was obeying the captain!

The secretary of General Keith Dryer, the commanding officer of Elmendorf Air Force Base, bolted into his office without the traditional knock. She knew he wouldn't mind. After all, this call was from none other than the President of The United States.

Seated alone near the last row of coach he sat quietly most of the flight with his head laid back as if to be pondering items of major importance.

Pastor Wright could barely see what had been going on. The drone of the jet engines near his seat, 22A, prevented him from hearing any of the commotion forward. But, something deep inside gave him a terrible uneasy feeling. He was sitting so far aft that the talk of what was happening never reached him. He had actually been sitting there with his eyes closed. He was not asleep. He was doing what he often does, praying.

He caught the attention of the two male flight attendants who were now flitting about the cabin in almost a state of panic. Their actions were inciting some passengers to think about an attempt to disarm the marshal. It was mostly talk, though.

"What's going on?" the pastor asks.

"The captain and an armed man are not letting a woman have an abortion. She wants it to take place. And if it doesn't happen, she's going to give birth right here on the airplane. It's just terrible! Can you do something?"

Neither Michael nor Harold knew that John was a pastor. They were encouraged when they watched him stand up and immediately head forward. Now there was someone who was going to do something about this. He looked authoritative - maybe he can stop this atrocious affair.

There was nothing in the way Pastor John Wright dressed that would indicate he was a minister. He was wearing slacks, a turtle neck shirt, and a sport coat.

He slowly slid open the First Class divider curtain and looked straight into the barrel of Frank Grafton's pistol.

"I wouldn't take one more step if I were you, buster."

"Sir, I am a minister, perhaps I can help."

Before Frank could react, Janie ran to Pastor Wright and took his hand.

"Pastor, maybe you can. This woman, her name is Erica, has told us she wants to have an abortion. There is a doctor on board who wants to perform one."

She continued, "The captain has taken a stand against it happening on the aircraft."

Then, "Could you speak with Erica?"

Erica was as reclined as far as the seat back would allow. Although still very uncomfortable, the labor pains had subsided the last five minutes. She was somewhat disoriented but was starting to regain her senses.

John sat down across the aisle from her. He had a smile that would melt an igloo. Many said it was part of his anointing, along with a crystal clear deep and kind voice.

"Erica, my name is John Wright. Can I speak with you?"

Erica's eyes opened with that quizzical look one has when they begin to recognize a voice. She turned her head and looked into Pastor Chuck's face. The quizzical look turned into a joyful one momentarily, then quickly showed extreme sadness as she turned away to the window.

"Erica, I would really like to help you in this difficult time." The pastor had noticed the recognition. His heart was touched.

For many years, John had been the pastor of one of the country's largest churches, Community Chapel of San Jose, California. What once began as a small bible study had burgeoned into mega church with thousands of people attending each week. They were drawn to his faithful teaching of the Bible, something he had never strayed from, even after many years in the ministry.

His heart for people never changed during the tremendous growth his church experienced. He was the same speaking in front of thousands and he was teaching six people in a small room. Today, however, his heart was heavy. Nearing sixty-five years old he recognized that he would soon retire, and must turn over the day-to-day pastoring of the church to another.

This was not going to be easy for Chuck. He wasn't worried about himself. He would have much to do if he desired – writing - speaking. His concern was for the church.

"Who would be the most able person to care for and continue to nurture the church," he would often ask himself.

There were many who vied for the position, some of whom pastored large churches themselves. Choosing the right man was an enormous burden.

He was on his way to Anchorage to speak at the Anchorage Center for Performing Arts. Over three-thousand people would soon be gathering to hear Pastor John Wright speak on the future - or lack thereof. The timing of the Abortion Protest Rally was perfect. It coincided with the grand opening of the "LTA" clinic.

"Erica, whatever your situation is, God is larger."

Frank marveled at the way this man seemed so confident of what needed to be said.

Erica's hands had been clutching each armrest. Her grip seemed to loosen. One hand even lifted as if asking to be held. John gently took that hand and held it within his own. Erica began to cry, and then weep, convulsively.

The Pastor instinctively placed his arm around her as she placed her tear stained face against his shoulder. It seemed to take five minutes before the sobbing stopped. There was no rush. There was something wonderful happening.

As the crying subsided Erica began to speak. "Pastor Chuck, I've attended your church."

She took a deep breath. "About 7 years ago a friend had taken me to a large meeting; it was like a rally. You spoke about current events and how they relate to biblical prophecy."

"Yes, Erica. For years we put on several rallies around the country." Pastor John could see that Erica was enjoying thinking about something other than her own huge problem.

"They were called 'Survival' rallies."

"Yes, now I remember," responded Erica. "They were about current events and how they relate to the end of the world."

"Well," John sought for the right words.

"I never liked the term 'end of the world.' It sounds so doom and gloom."

An eerie quiet had pervaded the scene. It was strange. In the middle of this huge and potentially violent conflict there suddenly emerges a strange calm, more like a peace, defying understand. Even the drone of the jet engines seemed to soften. At least, no one heard them now in First Class.

The buzz of activity continued in Coach, but here in First Class, it was like a different place, at a different time, under different circumstances.

The Pastor continued, "I like to think of it more like a grand entry of all the answers. It's what this world was created for in the first place."

Janie and Frank were now listening.

"The bible explains how this world, as we know it, was not intended to last forever. What happens next is going to be glorious!"

Frank couldn't resist a skeptic's question, "How do you get this from current events?"

John responded, "I can't think of one prophecy concerning the second coming of Jesus Christ that hasn't been fulfilled. "Wars and revolution literally cover the globe. We now have the return of diseases and sicknesses that don't respond to antibiotics and vaccines. These are all clearly related to what Jesus said in Matthew 24."

"For nation shall rise against nation, and kingdom against kingdom; and there shall be famines, and pestilences, and earthquakes, in various places."

Marshall Grafton spoke up.

"Wait a minute, there have always been diseases. There have always been wars!"

"That's true, " John went on, "but not to the extent there are today, especially with the marvelous medical breakthroughs we've known in recent history. And the medical community is stumped when it comes to solving these viruses that have returned - not to mention the AIDS virus. But there's much more."

John could sense that there was an ordained purpose to his being here at this place, at this precise moment. He remained obedient to what he felt God wanted him to do, and he continued:

"God gave us many signs to recognize the season of his return. Even though we don't know the day or the hour we should recognize the nearness of his coming."

All eyes were on the pastor...ears, too!

"He has instructed us to be ready, and understanding the prophecies helps us to be ready, and to be hopeful. In fact the bible refers to last day prophecy as the 'hope that purifies.' In other words, the looking and longing for the return of Jesus has an effect on us that is good."

The Pastor stopped speaking. He sensed that Erica wanted to say something.

"Pastor Chuck, the night I attended the rally you invited anyone who wanted to accept Jesus to do so. Well, I almost did."

Erica's face was now bright with enthusiasm. For these moments there was no pregnancy, no abortion, only a strange peace that permeated the First Class compartment occupied by only four people.

Her face began to show great sadness now as she thought about her present situation.

"A few years ago I just seemed to get caught up with the wrong person. He was an atheist and succeeded in having me question faith." Erica's tears had returned.

Janie, who had been listening intently, spoke up.

"Pastor, lately I've been asking a lot of questions concerning God. My husband and I went to a neighbor's home last week. This couple had such wonderful peace and joy. It was captivating. "

She continued, "My husband asked Larry why they seemed so happy. Larry asked his wife, Katie, to explain it to us. She simply said, " It's Jesus!"

Pastor John looked into Janie's eyes and knew the answer to the question he was about to ask.

"Janie, Jesus says that he stands at the door and knocks. He wishes to come into your heart - to take over your life. He wants you to trust him. Would you like to receive him now?"

Janie simply and softly replied, "Yes."

And there, somewhere above the skies over Southeast Alaska, 35000 feet closer to God, Janie closed her eyes, confessed her sins, and was born-again.

In the cockpit, Captain Ross was relieved that the last several minutes seemed calm. There had been no word of things back in the cabin and he reckoned that all had cooled down. Hopefully, nothing more would happen in flight. It would all happen in Anchorage.

There was so much emotion going on with Janie, Erica, and Pastor Chuck, that no one noticed the tears forming in Frank Grafton's eyes. No one until this large, muscular man knelt down in the aisle.

"Hey, I'm not going to get left out of this!" Frank tearfully declared.

Pastor John turned to Frank as if he had been totally expecting to.

"Frank, Jesus was the one who initiated the phrase 'born again. He was speaking with a religious leader of the day who had come to him secretly so he wouldn't be seen."

"Why secretly?" Frank asked.

"The religious leaders had rejected Him. They had gotten so caught up in religion that they were bound up in traditions and couldn't see that Jesus was the one they should have been waiting for all along."

"But, isn't religion good?" asked Frank.

"Yes, of course it is, but, not to the point that it separates you from the truth. There is a great old saying. It goes, 'Religion is Man's attempt to reach God. Christianity is God's attempt to reach Man'."

"What must I do?" Frank asked.

"There's no particular formula, no club to join. It's just a matter of asking God to forgive your sins, and then confessing your belief in Jesus as the Son."

"I don't know how. What words do I say?"

"Frank, if you will say these words, and, mean them in your heart, you can receive the Lord into your heart right now. Is that what you want?"

"Yes, I'm ready."

John led, "Dear Lord, I know that I am a sinner." Frank was repeating the words, hesitating slightly to consider each thing he would be saying.

"Forgive my sins."

"I know that you died on the cross for my sins."

"And I know that you later rose again."

" Lord, come into my life".

"Take over my life."

" Write my name into the Book of Life."

"Thank you, Lord Jesus. Amen."

At the "amen" this giant of a man slowly raised himself to his feet and looked upward.

"Praise you, Jesus!" he declared, remembering the days of a child being brought up in a Christian family.

Surprisingly, the first person to jump up and hug him was Erica. Soon, all four of them were wrapped in a giant hug, as much as a narrow aisle and seat arms would allow.

Back in Coach, however, the angst and chaos continued to reign. It was as if a simple soft curtain, that separated First Class from Coach, was now separating good and evil.

Chapter 10   San Francisco

The corporate headquarters of Pacific Airlines was a beautiful four story ivy lined brick building located just west of the airport and, despite its design, was only five years old.

Sam Pickering's luxurious office was on the top floor, in the northwest corner, and held a marvelous view of the San Francisco Bay. From there he could watch ferry boats, container ships, and keep an eye out on his beautiful sixty-two foot Pacemaker Yacht, The Midnight Sun.

Today was not a normal day at Pacific Airline's offices. There was a tension in the air as if something were amiss and out of kilter. The staff members felt it although only a few knew about Flight 571. It was just something in the air that was wrong, as if silent notes were being played off key. No-one spoke of it, but it was there.

Sam Pickering's office doors were normally open to simulate an open-door policy that didn't really exist. Today, they were closed and locked. Chief Pilot Rusty Ward was reaping the whirlwind of disfavor at not having succeeded in the change of command of Flight 571.

"Sam, I did all I could," Ward said defensively, "It's just that Ross Powers is a different breed, not a team player."

"I don't care what drives the man. I only want to get this thing fixed so we don't lose our close relationship with the F.A.A."

Just then, Pickering's phone rang. He had already directed his secretary to pass through only calls crucial to this situation. This call was from Noel Howard, the F.A.A. Administrator.

"Hello, Noel," Sam began, "we were just going over our options."

"Well, Sam, I don't exactly understand all the nuances of the President's involvement in this whole thing. What I do know is heads are going to roll if this doesn't work out well."

"We attempted to relieve Captain Powers of command of 571. No luck. The stubborn ox is on some sort of mission. He's totally irrational."

"So, we have," Howard continued, "a situation that is dangerous to passengers and public alike with some lunatic at the controls."

"I agree, Howard. Who knows what he might do?"

"What's the deal with the co-pilot?" Howard asked.

Chief Pilot Ward spoke up, "He's a total team player. If we could get him in command I'm sure everything would go as directed."

"Well then," Howard surmised, "we've got to get that airplane in his control. What did you say his name was?"

"Pearce, Damien Pearce." Offered Pickering, "And, by the way, he's my son-in-law!"

"Okay then. Check your manifests and search for passengers that might assist in a change of command."

"We'll get right on it. It will take a few moments to pull it up on the computer."

It took several minutes to pull out the passenger manifest from the computer. Rusty Ward had to run down the hall searching for someone who actually knew how to do it. A middle management type, a former operations agent, remembered the process. The printer began to print out passenger names and the seats they were in:

Alvarez, Sgt. J.	San Diego, CA	25D
Anderson, Miss N.	Everett, WA	12D
Bell, Dr. David	Redding, CA	2A
Glenn, Mr. D.	Auburn, WA	21F
Graves, Ms Paula	Los Angeles, CA	2F
Grafton, Frank	Lompoc, CA	21A
Hansen, Mr. R.	Tacoma, WA	15D
Hansen, Mrs. T.	Tacoma, WA	15F
Lambert, Mr. R	Los Angeles, CA	8F
Lawrence, Cpl W.	San Diego, CA	25A
Lewis, Miss H.	Everett, WA	12F
Mohns, Sgt. C.	San Diego, CA	25C
Moore, Miss F.	Everett, WA	12C

Owen, Miss R.	Everett, WA	12A
Paige, Ms. Erica	San Francisco, WA	8C
Powers, Draper	San Francisco, WA	18A
Rogers, Mrs. A.	Olympia, WA	15A
Rogers, (Enfant)	Olympia, WA	15B
Rogers, Mr. S.	Olympia, WA	15C
Wright, Chuck	San Jose, CA	22A
Zorn, Mr. R.	San Francisco, WA	19A
Zorn, Mrs. W.	San Francisco, WA	19C

After close examination, "Mr. Pickering, there are three passengers, with military sounding ranks, all seated together in row 25," the former agent reported.

"Okay! Check with reservations. Find out where their reservation came from. Perhaps we've found our help."

The research showed three marines: Sergeant J.D. "Doc" Alvarez, seat 25D, Sergeant C.L. "Chuck" Mohns, seat 25C, and Corporal W.W. "Bill" Lawrence, seat 25A.

After discovering their names and ranks, Noel Howard said, "I'll get word to Air Force One." F.A.A. Administrator Noel Howard was gone from the phone.

In the history of aviation there had never been a mutiny in which the commander of a public conveyance has been forcibly removed from command. Laws pertaining to mutinies were contained in Admiralty/Maritime Law, which related to mutinies at sea. There were heavy penalties for such an act, including death.

There are only a few federal laws and regulations, which explicitly prohibit passenger interference aboard aircraft. Federal Aviation Regulation 91.11 states that,

"No person may assault, threaten, intimidate, or interfere with a crewmember in the performance of the crewmember's duties aboard an aircraft being operated." Title 49, U.S Code, §46504 says that whoever, by assaulting or intimidating a flight crew member or flight attendant of an aircraft, interferes with the performance of their duties or lessens the ability of the crew member or flight attendant to perform their duties is subject to a fine and imprisonment for not more than 20 years. If a dangerous weapon is used in assaulting or intimidating the crewmember or flight attendant, the individual shall be imprisoned for any term of years or for life."

The ringing of his satellite phone startled Dr. Bell. He fidgeted with the phone to get it to answer. His anguished and irrational state of mind, still fuming over the events of the last hour, caused him to have difficulty operating the flip phone and getting it to answer. He rushed as much as he could in an attempt to silence the ringing so that word would not reach First Class.

Finally, "Yes?"

"Dr. Bell, this is George Evans. I'm President Jenson's Chief of Staff."

"Yes, George," Bell was almost whispering. "It's great you could get through."

"David, we might be able to solve the situation and get control of the aircraft from the crazed captain."

"How? How can you do it? What can I do?"

"The idea is to use three marines that are seated in Coach to overpower the captain."

"Then who will fly the plane?"

"There are two pilots in the cockpit. The co-pilot is a guy by the name of Damien Pearce. He will fly the plane."

"Will he go along with everything," the Doctor asked.

"Absolutely! He is the son-in-law of the airline's president. Now, give this phone to Sergeant Alvarez. He should be sitting in row 25. The three marines should be in uniform."

Without another word, Dr. Bell, concealing the small phone within his coat jacket, went aft to the last row in Coach. The three Marines were chatting away about their new assignment in Anchorage. They had not seen or heard the earlier commotion when Frank Grafton took charge of Erica half a fuselage away.

"Which one of you is Sergeant Alvarez?"

"That would be me, Sir."

Sergeant "Doc" Alvarez was twenty-seven years old. He stood over six feet tall and had the build of a professional weightlifter. The sight of this powerful man gave David Bell renewed hope that the plan could go through.

"Sergeant, this is a call for you from the White House."

"Yeah, right!"

"No, here, take the phone."

"This must be some kind of joke," decried the Sergeant.

He took the phone and pressed the earpiece to his head.

"Sergeant, this is no joke," George Evans stated firmly. "I am President Jenson's Chief of Staff and I have urgent instructions from your Commander in Chief."

"Sir, how do I know this isn't some prank?

"Sergeant, I can tell you that you are traveling with Sergeant Mohns and Corporal Lawrence to your new assignment at the Marine Corp Recruitment Center in

Anchorage. How could I know that if I wasn't who I said I was?"

"Okay, Sir. I'm convinced."

"Good. Now listen. I have some emergency instructions for you and your two companions."

Evans convinced the Marine that the flight was in the command of a madman and that their role was to devise a plan to overtake him and give aircraft command to First Officer Damien Pearce.

"I am putting Marine Major Joe Holtz on the phone. He will brief you as to the execution of the plan."

The Major began to describe the basics of the plan, which was to rush the cockpit door, which could easily be kicked in, and grab the arms of Captain Powers. They would immediately inform First Officer Pearce that he was now in command of the flight. Captain Powers was to be removed from his seat and restrained somewhere else in the plane.

Sergeant Alvarez began to brief Sergeant Mohns and Corporal Lawrence, both of who had been watching intently as the senior of the three listened on the phone.

As they started to rise, Dr. Bell asked, "Do you know about the armed man in First Class?"

"What? The man told me it was the captain who was armed," said Sergeant Alvarez.

"Well, actually, there is an armed man in First

Class that is cooperating with the captain. You will have to take care of him first."

Further refinements to the plan were developed. Alvarez would go first. He would peek through the curtain to ascertain the position of the armed man, and then signal the others. Then, the three of them would rush in and contain the situation in First Class. Once that was done, the cockpit would be next.

The three Marines walked to the curtain. Alvarez could see Frank Grafton sitting on the armrest of the aisle seat of row two. The pistol was in his holster strapped to his chest. With military style hand motions, Alvarez described the position and weapon situation. The element of surprise should guarantee the right outcome.

"One....two..."

At the count of "three" the three uniformed Marines, in single file, dashed through the curtain in a dead run.

"What...?"

Before Frank Grafton knew what was happening he was pinned to the floor and his weapon was removed. Pastor Chuck, Erica, and Janie were stunned by the sudden invasion and were powerless to act against the Marines, one of which pointed Frank's pistol in their direction.

"Don't make me use this. I'm under orders to take control of this aircraft. Stay exactly where you are!"

Mohns and Lawrence were holding Frank Marshal down.

"I'm a US Federal Marshal," Frank protested.

"I don't care who you are," replied Alvarez, "we're under orders."

"Search him. Make sure he has no other weapons."

The search of Frank Grafton provided no more weapons. However, a pair of handcuffs was found in the coat pocket, and a further search of pants pockets revealed the keys to those handcuffs. Frank was dealing with humiliation as well as anger. It was one thing to be surprised and overtaken . It was another to be restrained in your own handcuffs.

With Grafton adequately secured, Alvarez and Mohns were ready for the cockpit. Lawrence was to remain in First Class and contain the others.

The cockpit door crashed inward with a deafening "Bang" that sounded like a shotgun blast. Alvarez raced by the stunned boy, Draper, and grabbed a startled captain from behind and executed a painful and paralyzing chokehold. Ross's arms went up to fend off the attacker, but with every try, the chokehold tightened.

Mohns grabbed Draper and pushed him out of the cockpit and into First Class. The collapsed cockpit door was tossed out as well.

"Captain, put your arms down and I will release some pressure."

Ross was close to passing out, but was just conscious enough to obey.

He was out-numbered and had no opportunity to fight back. The chokehold was loosened a small bit, just enough for Ross's breathing to recommence.

"Pearce, you are now in command of this aircraft!"

First Officer Damien Pearce had also been initially shocked by the earthshaking events of the last sixty seconds. Soon, however, a glint of excitement shown in his face as he realized this was all for him. While still protecting the fractured fingers of his left hand, he unfastened his seat belt and reached over with his right and slapped Ross in the face, which surprised even the Sergeant who began to look at Pearce with questioning eyes.

"Keep this bastard out of my way!" Pearce commanded.

The chokehold had loosened just enough for Ross to start struggling again. Mohns came to Alvarez's aid and now both men were holding him and attempting to drag him out of his seat. This would necessitate yanking him across the center pedestal where many important items of flight were located. As they did, Ross legs were thrashing about as a natural function from the sense of being strangled.

The 737's center pedestal between the two pilot seats contains the controls for essential items of flight. This forward, slightly raised, section of the pedestal contains the flap handle, speedbrake handle, trim indicator, and fuel shutoff valves.

The most critical controls on this center pedestal are the fuel shutoff valves, two small handles that serve to control fuel to the engines. They are raised to the "run" position during the start process, and they are lowered to the shutoff position during engine shutdown at the gate after a flight. In the "run" position there is a detent that prevents the valves from slipping out of position, a dangerous proposition that could shut an engine down inadvertently in flight.

As Ross was being manhandled out of his seat his right shoe clipped the fuel shutoff valves and broke off both valve handles from the pedestal. The right engine valve broke off with the actual control position remaining in "run." However, the left engine valve was broken off subsequent to an instantaneous hook of the shoe, pulling the valve handle downward before it completely broke off. The left engine spun down and quit.

There was instant pandemonium in the cockpit as the two Marines succeeded in removing the captain from his seat. As they held Ross down on the floor of the cockpit, overhead-warning lights illuminated. The 737 swerved toward the left at the loss of the left engine and the loud "auto-pilot disconnect" warning horn, which sounds almost like a submarine's dive signal, immediately sounded. The auto-pilot, normally on for the entire cruise portion of the flight, disconnected. The autopilot is designed to disconnect if the control forces opposing it reach a certain force. Since the airplane turned left at the loss of the engine the autopilot could not control to the heading to which it had been programmed. Therefore, it just lets go and pilots must take manual control.

However, this chaos, which requires quick thinking by pilots, combined with Damien 's basic weak flying skills, left the newly appointed "pilot-in-command" in a confused and bewildered state of mind.

"Get control of the airplane!" Sergeant Alvarez yelled above the noise.

"C'mon man," Mohns added, "Are you trying to kill us all?"

Even Ross, who was still being held down, managed to scream, "Pearce, grab the yoke, put in right rudder!"

Somewhere back in Pearce's mind, actual directions being yelled in his direction seemed familiar. During his initial training this was a common event to prevent him from wrecking the small trainer and killing both himself and the instructor. It was enough to make Pearce respond by doing exactly what Ross had yelled from behind.

"Now, click off the autopilot warning horn on the yoke!"

Ross now yelled at his attackers, "Let me up, you want him flying this thing?"

The two sergeants were about ready to release Ross when they began to sense that the co-pilot was beginning to take control. They continued to hold Ross down.

Pearce managed to get the aircraft under control by adding sufficient right rudder to counteract the left turn. The rudders are controlled with foot pedals. Pearce had two good feet, but only one good hand. With one hand on the yoke he began to steer the aircraft to its earlier heading and was allowing the plane to descend in order to maintain its flying speed with the loss of one engine.

The Boeing 737, as all commercial jets, cannot maintain adequate flying speed with the loss of half power at the higher altitudes, and must descend to lower altitudes to allow for slower airspeeds. This aerodynamic principle is a function of the air being thicker, or more dense, at lower altitudes, which provides more lift to the wings. Ross directed Pearce to let the aircraft descend below twenty thousand feet.

A pilot's legs can tire from pushing in on a rudder pedal for too long, so a rudder trim mechanism is available to relieve the rudder pressure and configure the aircraft for the out-of-trim condition. Pearce was able to turn the rudder trim, located on the aft portion of the center pedestal, with the palm of his damaged left hand. He moaned in pain during the process but succeeded in adjusting the trim. The aircraft, now back in control, had resumed its course to Anchorage and still in a descent. With the aircraft trimmed out for its situation the autopilot could now be engaged again.

"If you're not going to let me fly, at least set me up to help keep this guy from killing us," Ross suggested.

After conferring for a few seconds, the Marines decided that, if they could adequately restrain Ross, they would allow him back in his seat. While Alvarez continued to hold Ross down, Mohns was sent to the back to find something to tie the captains arms and hands. After a brief search he found the seat belts and buckles that are used by the flight attendants before takeoff to demonstrate their use.

Both men then controlled Ross as he was allowed back in his seat. Then, the belts were used to tie Ross's arms to his sides so he could not interfere with Pearce's control of the aircraft. Secretly, both Marine sergeants were having second thoughts about the ability of this First Officer to fly this now damaged aircraft. If push came to shove, at least this captain, who they still considered a rogue, could be released to save their lives.

ATC had been attempting to call the aircraft on the radio. The previous confusion in the cockpit resulted in them not being answered. Now they were calling again.

"Pacific 571, Pacific 571, Anchorage Center. You were not cleared for descent!"

With the autopilot now engaged Damien Pearce, with a trembling right hand, was finally able to pick up the microphone. He keyed the transmit button.

"This is Pacific 571. We have an emergency"

"Roger, Pacific 571. Say type of emergency."

"We have lost one engine and are now descending. We must get on the ground. What's the nearest airport?"

"You're halfway between Sitka and Yakutat. Juneau would be about the same distance back as well."

"Okay, I'll get right back to you."

Damien needed some time to think, but the last thing he wanted was input from Powers. Ross was compelled to try.

"Listen, Pearce, this plane should…." He was interrupted.

"Powers, I am in command and I will decide where we land!"

"Okay, but you should consider something."

Pearce was having trouble making up his mind as to the shortest destination and did not interrupt Ross this time.

"Look, you've got tailwinds. That means it will take more time to turn around and go to Sitka or Juneau. Yakutat is closer. Besides, it has straight in approaches."

Ross was alluding to the demanding approaches at Sitka and Juneau due to the topography near both airports. The approaches required maneuvers around high terrain and therefore could not include vertical guidance, with a glide slope, to the runway. They were challenging to pilots, especially those of an airline that did not serve those airports regularly. They were listed in Pacific Airlines' Operation Specifications as "Provisional," to be used only in need, for fuel or emergencies. Therefore, the charts for those airports were included in the chart manuals of Pacific pilots.

Pacific Airlines did not serve Yakutat either, but the charts showed that an ILS approach was available. Ross reasoned that Pearce could handle a single-engine approach to an ILS easier than a non-precision one which required more talent than Ross figured Pearce had.

"Look, let me fly the airplane. I will get us safely

on the ground." Ross said to the two men restraining him."

Damien flew into a rage. His eyes were on fire and he began to shake with anger.

"Shut-up! You are not only relieved of command; you are apparently under arrest as well. I am fully capable of completing this flight."

After ordering the Marines to prepare to remove Powers from the seat again if he continues to interfere, Damien keyed the microphone again.

"Center, give us vectors to Juneau."

"Roger, Sir. The weather at Juneau has been below minimums all day. However, it has improved in the last thirty minutes to bare minimums. It goes up and down."

Ross was incredulous and silently shook his head in disgust. Sergeants Alvarez and Mohns were growing more concerned at the decision-making capability of the pilot they had been responsible for placing in control.

The sudden swerve of the aircraft had sent passengers into a panic. Harold and Michael had sat down in an empty row of seats and had long since given up responsible roles as crewmembers of Pacific Flight 571. Paula Graves stood up and declared in that loud annoying voice that only she could muster above the noise of the aircraft.

"Everyone, keep quiet. Stay in your seats!"

Paula decided to walk forward and investigate. She had yet to learn of the successful authorized mutiny and was delighted to see David Bell and an armed Marine in control in First Class. Through the busted down cockpit door she could see two uniformed Marines in control in the cockpit. She joined David Bell who was approaching Erica Paige. Bell ordered Corporal Lawrence to move Frank Grafton, Pastor Chuck, and Janie away from Erica. They complied.

Bell approached a frightened Erica.

"Erica, I have great news. We are now able to perform the abortion. I have everything I need."

"Get away from me," she cried out. "I don't want an abortion. I want to have this baby!"

"You're hysterical, Erica. Just calm down."

"No! You're crazy. Get away from me." She was screaming.

"Paula, help me hold her. She needs a sedative to calm her down."

Erica began to fight with all her might as Dr. Bell and Paula Graves wrestled her back into the seat, from which she was trying to emerge. Erica managed to kick Bell in the groin, causing him to yell out in pain.

Paula smacked her hard across the face. Bell was furiously trying to load the hypodermic needle with a strong sedative that would render Erica unconscious. He had no anesthesia; the sedative would have to do. However, the abrupt movments of the airplane almost caused him to inject himself. He decided to give up and try when things settled down.

"Pacific 571, Roger. You're cleared direct Sisters VOR.

"Roger, Center. Also, please advise company that Captain Pearce is in control of the aircraft."

"Yes sir, Captain Pearce."

Ross couldn't believe the arrogance of Pearce to refer to himself as "Captain Pearce." He was also inflamed that Pearce had chosen Juneau for an emergency landing.

Juneau's airport wind would require an approach from the west and a landing on Runway 8, which lay just east of a large hill. Part of the hill had been shaved off to permit an aircraft to stay lower when passing. This shave-off was called the "Cut," and was familiar to pilots flying into and out of Juneau.

Ross knew about the Cut having flown light airplanes into Juneau for fishing trips. The approach chart did not describe the Cut adequately and Ross knew he'd have to brief Pearce about it sooner or later. However, Pearce was not allowing Ross to speak at all.

"Pacific 571, I show you thirty miles from the Sisters vor now. You are cleared to descend to nine thousand."

Pilots return for recurrent training on an annual basis. At the completion of two days simulator training, they receive a Proficiency Check, which allows them to return to the line. The training and check rides emphasize maneuvers in an engine failure situation. Actual engine failures almost never occur. In regular line flying, an engine out situation normally resulted from a purposeful cautionary shutdown. An engine failure would result in a whole new set of emergency checklists. Flight 571 had an engine failure, which was unable to be restarted, and those checklists would not be executed today under the command of Damien Pearce.

Over the years, Damien Pearce managed to squeak by the checkrides only because he was related to the president of the airline. No instructor wanted to be the one to "bust" the president's son-in-law, and therefore gave Pearce the benefit of every doubt at check ride time. Pearce did possess enough skill, with some coaching, to do a minimal job at the maneuvers, enough that the check pilots rationalized would get him by. They all reckoned that Damien would have a difficult time eventually checking out as captain, but decided to deal with that dilemma when the time came.

With the autopilot on, the pilot's task was to program it properly for the approach. When it came to automation, Pearce had adequate talent. This served him in training as well in that, if he could keep the aircraft on the autopilot, his weak flying skills would be less detected. An autopilot could be kept on in a precision approach, an ILS. However, the problem with Juneau, and every non-precision approach, is that the autopilot must eventually be turned off and the aircraft manually flown for the last few hundred feet. Juneau required hand flying below five hundred feet.

"Pacific 571, you're cleared for the LDA approach, Runway 8."

An LDA stands for Localizer Displaced Approach. In an LDA the localizer, normally providing horizontal guidance in a straight line of flight to the runway, is displaced off at an angle. This is required because the terrain out from the airport would not allow a straight in approach. Therefore, after flying in at an angle, the pilots would have to readjust the direction of the aircraft to land on the runway. Juneau's localizer provided guidance along a horizontal track of sixty-two degrees. The runway, however, on the back side of the "Cut," was eighty degrees. This meant that almost a twenty-degree change was necessary just above the runway. Crosswinds, common at Juneau, could affect that amount of heading change required, sometimes making it worse.

The LDA approach to Juneau was difficult

enough for an airplane with all engines operating normally. Today's approach with one engine out would be demanding for even an exceptionally qualified pilot.

"Damien, this is ridiculous. You should let me fly this approach."

"Shut-up!"

"Damien, the weather's not good enough for this approach."

"Can you guys put a rag in his mouth?"

The marines were growing more and more concerned at what Ross had been saying. They didn't respond to Pearce. They were beginning to be afraid.

Damien remained silent as the airplane departed Sisters VOR on a course to intercept the final approach course to the airport.

"You need to descend to 5500 feet," instructed Ross.

Damien didn't object. When someone is not keeping up with the demands of the flying, it is said he is "behind the airplane." Damien was so far "behind the airplane" that even he was starting to get nervous. The Marines noticed.

The autopilot was adequately controlling the aircraft horizontally without additional inputs from Damien. However, this approach required step-down descents after brief level-offs at certain spots. The pilot had to continually reset the altitudes and vertical rates to keep the aircraft on the proper profile, a crucially important factor in this mountainous environment.

Descents and level-offs required changes in power. So far the auto-throttles, used in conjunction with the autopilot, were handling the job. However, power changes also brought about changes in the degree of rudder needed to counteract the differential thrust of only one engine.

"More rudder!"

Then, "Less Rudder!"

Ross was trying his best to keep everyone alive but the restraints on his arms were prohibiting anything but instruction.

"Guys," Ross pleaded with the Marines, "If you don't loosen these straps, you might not live through this!"

Sergeant Alvarez was very tempted to release the captain. He held back. Damien Pearce appeared to be in some sort of trance. He was complying with the directions from Ross not objecting to the instruction.

"Damien, don't go to minimums. If you need to miss, it will be extremely difficult with one engine."

As the aircraft passed Barlo Intersection, a chart depicted point, Damien reached for the vertical speed dial of the autopilot. He dialed it down to fifteen hundred feet per minute rate of descent, and had placed the altitude selector at one thousand feet, as directed by the chart.

During this descent, however, Damien forgot to let up on the rudder trim, and the auto-pilot, unable now to keep up with the out-of-trim condition, clicked off. The loud warning horn went off again which frightened Sergeant Alvarez. Instinctively, he released the belts holding Captain Powers' arms.

Ross immediately grabbed the yoke with one hand, and the throttle to the one good engine with the other. He shoved the throttle forward to its maximum thrust position, at the same time gently pulling back the yoke. In a magnificent coordinated move, Ross's right foot depressed just the right amount of rudder to provide for a perfect in-trim missed approach. As the aircraft laboriously climbed, an immediate right turn was begun as well to comply with the missed approach procedures, and get away from mountains.

Ross was back in control. The Sergeants breathed a sigh of relief, and were actually thankful for Ross's abilities. Damien sat still, unwilling to physically confront Ross again. Once an adequate and safe altitude was reached Ross confidently picked up the microphone.

"Anchorage Center, this is Pacific 571."

Ross went on, "We've just missed at Juneau. We'll take initial vectors to Yakutat."

"Yes, Sir, Captain Pearce," the controller

responded mistakenly, "Turn right heading two seven zero."

"Roger, and by the way, this is Captain Ross Powers."

The twisting and turning of the aircraft had made it impossible for Dr. Bell to prepare for the abortion. He took a seat next to the unconscious young woman and waited until he thought things would calm down. He had no idea that the aircraft movements were caused by an "aborted" attempt to land at Juneau. Everyone else had strapped in when the airplane started moving erratically. Corporal Lawrence sat in the last seat of First Class with his pistol at the ready.

Following the missed approach, however, Sergeants Alvarez and Mohns came out of the cockpit.

"What's going on," asked the Corporal? "Why aren't you guarding the captain?"

"It's all over, Bill," replied Alvarez, "We've allowed the captain to be back in command. The co-pilot almost killed us all. Let's just forget this so-called order from the White House. I'd rather be alive!"

Alvarez took the gun from Lawrence and handed it back to Marshal Grafton.

"Sorry, Marshal. It looks like we were given some bum information."

"That's okay, Sergeant. You were only following

orders. Stay with us up here in First Class."

Erica Paige was beginning to awaken. Frank went to her seat and ordered Bell, sitting there in shock, to Coach. He also pointed the gun right into Paula's face.

"And now, Bitch. Get out of my sight!"

Paula Graves was speechless for the first time in her life. She quickly moved into the aisle and back into Coach.

Frank looked at Pastor Chuck, sheepishly.

"Sorry about my language, Pastor."

"That's okay, Frank. I was thinking the same thing."

With one engine out, the performance of the 737 was severely hampered. It would fly okay, but could only climb to seventeen thousand feet.

"Anchorage Center, Pacific 571 requesting one-seven-thousand for an altitude to Anchorage."

"Roger, 571, climb to and maintain one-seven-thousand."

After leveling off, and turning on the autopilot, Ross finally had some time to analyze the center control panel that housed the broken fuel levers. He noted that the levers had been broken off just inside the slots from which they had originally protruded.

He thought, "If I could just get behind that panel,

there may be enough lever left to raise, and get the left engine started again."

Damien Pearce turned and watched as Ross, having pulled his Leatherman tool from his flight kit, began to loosen screws near where the levers once were. Soon, a metal plate was removed, revealing a one-eighth inch stub of the fuel levers for each engine, one in the up-run position, and one in the down-cutoff position. All that would be required to start the left engine would be to raise that left engine lever after turning on the ignition with the left engine start switch.

Ross placed the left start switch to the "on" position. As the engine rpm increased to 20%, Nathan took the pliers part of his Leatherman, and pulled the stub of the #1 start lever to the up-run position. Immediately, Ross saw that the Exhaust Gas Temperature (EGT) gauge was rising, indicating that the engine had received the fuel and was starting.

"Anchorage Center, we've restored our other engine, and can now accept flight level 350 (Thirty-five thousand feet)

"Roger, 571. Good job. Climb to and maintain Flight Level 350. Shall we cancel the "Emergency?"

"Affirmative, Center, and change our destination back to Anchorage. We're basically back to normal." Ross felt no need to involve ATC in the situation in the cabin.

"Roger, 571, you're re-cleared to Anchorage via direct Yakutat, J501 Anchorage."

After the roller-coaster-type ride on the approach to Juneau, the flight had now settled down under Ross's control. It began to quiet down in the cabin as previous fears subsided. Everyone was waiting - wondering - what events would occur upon their arrival into Anchorage.

Erica Page, after being silent for a long time, touched Pastor John on the hand. As he leaned over, she softly said:

"Pastor Chuck, for the last hour I have been praying silently and asking God to forgive me."

As she continued, her eyes reflected a calm and peace that she hadn't known for many years.

"I've decided to not have an abortion. I will deliver this child and let some wonderful family adopt him or her." She glanced in Janie's direction, and winked.

"You've made a wonderful decision, Erica. And I'm sure that God is very happy to have you back in his arms. His love for you had never changed." Pastor Chuck's smile reassured Erica that she would not have to go it alone.

In the cockpit Ross sat pensively staring straight ahead. Draper had returned to the seat behind his father. Damien Pearce stared glumly out his right window. Now, in the darkness Ross pondered his fate and questioned his decisions in the whole affair.

Suddenly, as if he'd asked silent questions, silent answers seemed to appear out of nowhere, into his heart. He thought of scriptures he had learned years ago. He also thought it was strange that they would occur to him now:

"Trust in the Lord with all your heart, and lean not into your own understanding. In all your ways acknowledge him and he shall direct your paths."

And. *"They that wait upon the Lord will renew their strength. They will…"*

Back in coach, David Bell became more and more anguished.

"Paula, I have a gun."

"You do? Well, why haven't you used it, you coward?"

"I've never used it before."

"Give it to me, you raving idiot."

"Uh..uh…I'm not sure."

"Bell, you are the most lily-livered wimp I've ever seen. If you don't give me that gun, I personally am going to beat the crap out of you!"

Bell was shocked by the threatening words coming from an attractive face. However, the eyes revealed that this medium sized woman might just back up her threat. Man or woman, David Bell was highly intimidated.

"What are you going to do?" as he handed the 38 to Graves.

"Just shut-up, you..." Even Paula Graves could think of no adequate adjectives.

"I will now take charge of this situation!"

She took off for the cockpit in a full out run. She did not take notice of the cockpit door laying halfway in the galley and partially sticking out into the aisle leading to the cockpit. She tripped over the door's end and fell forward into the cockpit.

Her momentum carried her almost into Pearce's lap.

"BANG!" The sound of a gunshot was unmistakable.

"KAPLASH!" It was the sound of glass breaking, as the two thick panes of the window in front of First Officer Pearce shattered.

"WHOOSH!" The explosive sound of air as the right, forward, cockpit window disappeared. The initial sound was that of air being sucked out of the rapidly depressurizing jet. Everything, in the cockpit, not strapped in tight, was immediately sucked out through the large opening: maps, glasses, kits, checklists...

and one human being.

"PLOOSH!" The sound of the woman being sucked through the window was one Ross would never forget. Her hips had lodged in the opening for a few seconds, momentarily stopping the vacuum.

Ross instinctively grabbed both of her legs in an attempt to pull her back into the cockpit. The upper half of Paula Graves was flapping like a rag-doll, back and forth on the top of the fuselage, just above the cockpit. Ross could see Graves' head being beat against the small upper window.

He continued to yank desperately on the legs. Damien Pearce had been knocked unconscious when hit on the head by the knees of Paula Graves as she flew towards the open window.

Then, "SLOOSH." The force of the vacuum finally succeeded in sucking the rest of Paula Graves through the opening, in-spite of Ross's grip. In a flash, she was gone, her body falling thousands of feet in a vertical plunge to the icy waters below.

Ross grabbed his oxygen mask from its holder and placed it over his face. He also started to place another oxygen mask over the face of co-pilot Pearce. However, he noticed a small gunshot wound just below the left ear. The bullet had penetrated Pearce's neck before careening into the windshield.

One bullet had resulted in the deaths of two people. And, it had placed this jet in great jeopardy.

After quickly determining that Draper had also donned the mask that had fallen from the ceiling of the cockpit, just above where he was sitting. Ross pulled the throttles back, the speedbrake up, and pushed the nose over to dive for a lower altitude, somewhere below ten-thousand feet, where he and the others could breath.

The oxygen system was only designed for several minutes use, just enough to allow crew and passengers to breath until the aircraft could get to a much lower altitude.

Papers and light objects in the cabin had begun to rush forward toward the cockpit at the initial explosion, and followed Paula Graves through the opening where the windshield once was. Fortunately, most everyone in the cabin had their seat belts on, or was able to grab onto something stationary.

The gun had flown out of Paula Graves's hand by the force of the kickback, and had landed back beside Bell, who had managed to grab it again. With his free hand, he donned the small oxygen mask, one of one hundred and thirty-six that had deployed throughout the cabin. Everyone else in coach, and First Class, was breathing from a mask also.

Back in the cockpit, Ross was fighting to keep his mask on, as the out-rush of air had been replaced by a torrent of in-coming wind as the aircraft became totally depressurized. The faster the airplane was flying, the larger force of air was rushing in around Ross, hampering his ability to even move his arms. To slow the speed of the aircraft would have lowered the rate of vertical descent, which would have increased the time to get to a safe altitude. Ross continued to push the yoke forward to keep the plane coming down.

The altimeter was spinning down.

33,000'

29,000'

25,000'

20,000'

It seemed to take forever. It was only taking seconds.

16,000'

12,000'

Ross began to pull back on the yoke so as to level off at 10,000', where there was safe, breathable air. As he pulled back, the speed of the aircraft began to slow as well.

11,000'

11,500'

10,000'

Ross was now able to let the plane continue to slow to its minimum speed, without flaps, of two hundred and ten knots. Still, the sound of the rushing air sounded like a continuous cannon roar. It would have to remain that way for the remainder of the flight.

Physical movement was more unrestrictive now and Ross could turn and check on Draper. After getting a thumbs-up signal from his son he removed the now-unneeded oxygen mask. Draper followed, and then immediately returned both hands to his ears. Ross looked around for something to stuff in his ears to help lessen to deafening noise, but could find nothing.

They were still forty minutes out of Anchorage. They had passed Yakutat earlier and Ross thought about turning around. However, Anchorage provided much longer runways and, by the time they would reverse course and maneuver for an approach into Yakutat, they could be in the Anchorage area.

The route to Anchorage is westerly. From their present position there would be no high mountain ranges to cross. Ross was familiar enough with the area to know that he was staying primarily over water, the Gulf of Alaska. Further along, the little actual terrain they would be crossing was at lower altitudes, no threat to an aircraft flying at ten thousand feet above sea level.

"Pacific 571, this is Anchorage Center."

ATC had seen the aircraft go into a dive and had been trying desperately to contact them.

"Pacific 571, Pacific 571, Do you hear Anchorage Center?"

The noise continued at such a deafening level that communication with ATC was impossible. The scope in Anchorage Center's radar room had shown the readout of the target as the numbers representing the altitude declined.

"They're going down!" The controller had thought they were going to crash.

The supervisor ran to the nervous controller and stood behind him as the frantic calls continued.

"Pacific 571! Pacific 571! Do you read Anchorage Center."

Still nothing. Just numbers on a screen, showing the dive. Then, the pace of the number changes began to slow.

"Wait, I think they're leveling off." The controller was excited.

"They are! They've leveled at ten thousand feet!"

The supervisor now keyed his mike, "Pacific Flight 571, we show you level at ten thousand feet. Please acknowledge."

Still nothing.

Ross couldn't even hear the controllers due to the noise of the air rush. He had slowed the aircraft even further by extending flaps. They were flying now at one hundred and fifty knots. Still, there was too much noise to hear and speak. Ross reached down to the transponder and dialed in 7700.

The transponder transmits a code to ATC, which shows up with the "blip" on the screen representing the aircraft. It is used to identify each aircraft so adequate separation can be accomplished. It also transmits a "Mode C," which provides the controllers with altitude readouts. All aircraft, receiving their initial clearances, are provided with a distinct 4-digit code. Special codes were preserved for emergency conditions.

If an airliner was being hijacked, and the pilot was prohibited by the hijackers from communicating to ATC, the transponder could be covertly used to get the message to the controllers. Pilots have been trained to dial "7600" into the transponder, hopefully, without being observed by the hijackers. Upon reading a "7600" on the screen, the controller would be "in the loop," and appropriate measures could take place.

"7700" was assigned for all other general emergencies.

"Hey!" The controller was ecstatic. "They're squawking '7700.' They're okay! They're still flying!"

A roar of joy swept through Anchorage Center's radar room, which accommodated eight controllers at various screens. Every controller had been fearful of the loss of Pacific Flight 571.

"Pacific 571, do you hear Anchorage Center now? The controller kept trying. "They're still not answering."

"There must be something wrong with their radios. Continue transmitting," directed the supervisor.

"Pacific Flight 571, I still don't hear you. In case you're hearing me, you are still cleared to Anchorage. The winds favor runway 6R."

His transmissions were in vain. Ross could not hear anything, even after turning his speakers up to the highest volume level. Ross was heading to Anchorage. He knew that ATC would know to clear the airways for him. He didn't know that the military had already taken full control of the airport and that all other aircraft would be diverted for different reasons; reasons that related to the "special" treatment in store for Pacific Airlines Flight 571.

At one hundred and fifty knots, the buffeting of the aircraft, that had been very heavy at higher speeds, had subsided. It had resulted from the unusual airflow entering the cockpit from the right front window, affecting the aerodynamic qualities of the 737. At this slower speed, however, the aircraft handle much more normally, except for the roar of the air.

Soon, the Anchorage Airport came into view. Everyone in the airplane, in-spite of the noise and rushing air throughout the cabin, was encouraged at the sight. Ross examined the terrain for signs of the wind direction, which would dictate which runway to use.

Airplanes take off and land into the wind. Airspeed, not groundspeed, determines the lift available for flight. Therefore, going into the wind during takeoff and landing provided more airspeed. Ross remembered, from the weather package he received at the flight's beginning, that the wind had favored a landing on either of the two runways heading in a magnetic direction of 060 degrees. Anchorage had two parallel runways, six-left and six-right. Six-right was the longest so Ross elected to enter the traffic pattern for that runway.

His down-wind leg would take him along side of the runway, about two miles out. He then planned a right, ninety-degree, "base-leg" turn, followed by a last ninety-degree right turn to the final approach. He would give himself a long "final" to allow the aircraft to be "stabilized" far enough out to ensure a successful approach and landing with this wounded bird.

On "downwind" leg he looked to his left and right to determine there were no other aircraft in the area. He reasoned that the absence of any other flights in the area was because of the emergency classification of Pacific 571. What he didn't realize was that, long before the emergency of a depressurized aircraft with a blown out windshield, the military, under the command of General Keith Dryer, had secured the entire airport, canceling operations of any other aircraft, departing or arriving.

General Dryer had begun his military career as a student at the Air Force Academy in Colorado Springs. His appointment was by a local congressman that had been elected largely because of the financial help of Keith Dryer's father.

"Tiger, take a lesson from all this," his father would lecture. "Knowing the right people can pave the way for success."

Keith hated being called "Tiger." It made him feel inadequate, that he could not live up to his father's expectations and was forever bent on getting his dad's approval. Keith Dryer's father was a real go-getter. His success in the real estate field had brought great wealth.

"Father," the letter had begun, "...I don't know how much more of this I can take! The hazing is so mean and my feelings get hurt all the time. Can I just come home?"

If Keith thought the hazing was difficult it was nothing compared to the reaction from his father. The phone call came within 10 minutes after the letter was received.

"You will NEVER amount to anything," his father was screaming. "I've always known you couldn't hack it. If you don't stay in there you will embarrass me in front of all my friends, including the political contacts that got you appointed there in the first place!"

After some silent delay. "I'm sorry, Father. It was just a momentary reaction. I'll be fine. In fact, they are considering me for class officer." He was lying.

"Now, that's my 'Tiger' talking. That's more like it! We'll just forget this ever happened. See you at Christmas Break."

Keith Dryer was now out of options. He had to succeed at the academy, at any cost. He was able to stick out the first year from just the fear of invoking his father's wrath.

Things began to approve in his second year. There was no more hazing. There was, however, a significant increase in the difficulty of some classes. Math related subjects had never been Keith's strong point and second year Calculus was about ready to destroy an already only mediocre grade point average. It was also difficult for several other cadets. In fact, there were several classes that had many cadets worried about getting through.

Keith has only one friend. His name was Cadet Tom Jenner. They came up with a devious plan involved an extremely complex method of providing test questions to others after the initial groups took the tests. Since the

Academy operated on the honor system, whereby the cadets are trusted to refrain from any dishonest activity, the plan could be executed right under the noses of the faculty.

It seemed foolproof and had drawn in over one hundred cadets by the time Keith had entered his junior year. What made it even more incredible, Tom Jenner was Honor Captain, the cadet charged with making sure the honor system wasn't abused. When Tom graduated one year ahead of Keith he ensured that Keith would be his successor. This scheme had actually become financially rewarding. Keith assumed the Honor Command at the beginning of his senior year.

Near Thanksgiving, Keith could see that the lid was about to blow over the cheating. He could see that a huge scandal could begin at any moment. It was time for him to take action. Keith Dryer blew the whistle on the entire cheating activity. He did it in such a way as to keep himself totally unscathed by the scandal. In fact, he was elevated in the eyes of the faculty and administration by uncovering the entire cheating process.

By the time the anvil fell, and the scandal roared, the individuals involved had been summarily released by the academy. All except Keith Dryer. For the remainder of his senior year he worried about the possibility of his own incrimination. But it never occurred. He was home free.

He graduated, with honors, at the expense of ruined lives and careers. Even distinguished military commanding officers of the academy were forced to resign over the scandal. Months later, Tom Jenner was found behind a Bachelor Office Quarters at Luke AFB, dead, by his own hand.

Lessons learned from his father, and later through the academy, paved the way for a rapid progression up the ranks. At every step Keith Dryer's father was there to encourage. He had one desire for his son and that was for him to one day become Chairman of the Joint Chiefs of Staff.

Ten miles out on final approach, as Pacific 571 descended through three thousand feet, Ross reached over and brought the gear lever from its neutral position to the down position. In spite of the continuing air noise, those in the back could hear the main landing gear come out of their retracted positions in the belly of the aircraft. The sound provided additional encouragement that this nightmare of a flight would soon be over.

As the main and nose gear indicator lights indicated a "down and locked" position, Ross selected twenty-five degrees of flaps and slowed the aircraft to one hundred and forty knots. Then he selected thirty degrees of flaps and slowed to one hundred and thirty knots. He had planned to use forty degrees of flaps to allow the aircraft to land at the slowest possible airspeed of one hundred and twenty-eight knots.

The wind at the airport was reported at 090 degrees at a speed of twenty knots. Ross did not know the exact velocity and direction of the wind, but had noted smoke from a factory, and dust on the ground, that showed this experienced pilot the general direction and speed. Instinctively, he knew that a 20 to 30 degree crosswind from the right would occur on landing. As the aircraft passed over Fire Island, just five miles west of the runway, Ross calculated that the "crabbing" of the aircraft's path, a necessary adjustment to the heading to keep it moving straight towards the runway, confirmed the crosswind and approximate velocity.

General Dryer had been taught that warfare advantages could be enhanced by an enemy's perception of the opposition's strong military presence. He had ordered two fast moving tanks to take up positions along both sides of Runway 6-right, near the expected landing area of Pacific 571. They were further instructed to begin moving in advance of the approaching aircraft in order to stay ahead of it during the landing and rollout.

"The madman at the controls will cower at our mere presence," the General said. "That's what we learn at the Academy," He boasted.

Ross had now slowed the 737 to its final approach speed as he neared the runway. Crossing the threshold of the runway he began to flare. Just then, from somewhere to the right of the aircraft, dust and dirt was being thrown into the air, so much so that he couldn't see that it was coming from a tank moving alongside the runway.

Because the wind was coming from that direction, the tracks of the fast moving tank were kicking up much dust and dirt which was now being blown onto the runway and in front of the approaching 737.

Just twenty feet above the runway the cockpit suddenly filled with flying clouds of dirt. Some of it entered directly into Ross's eyes. The pain was excruciating, blinding him. Ross was tempted to remove his hands from the controls to comfort his eyes but knew that would be instant death for all aboard. He couldn't land in the blind. That would be just as dangerous. The only course of action was to initiate a go-around.

He shoved the throttles forward and began to pull back on the yoke when he suddenly realized that his blindness from the large amount of dirt lodged in both eyes would prevent him from seeing his own instruments. He could not see how much he was pulling back. He could not see his airspeed, which was mandatory to keep the aircraft in the air. He could not see where he was going. In an instant he realized that they were probably going to crash.

Suddenly, there was a voice in his ear. It was that of his son, Draper.

"You're pitched up to thirty degrees. Lower your nose a bit. Good!"

Ross complied with the instructions.

"Your airspeed is one hundred and fifty, and you're climbing through one thousand feet."

Ross immediately realized that Draper, who had been able to fly the 737 simulator several times, had instinctively recognized his father's dilemma, and was now providing enough information to keep this thing in the air.

Draper had accompanied his dad on several occasions when the HUD II was being tested in the simulator. Once the testing was complete Ross would put Draper in the seat and give him some basic instruction in flying the 737. It had all been for fun, and Ross had not recognized how seriously Draper had taken the opportunities, or how proficient his young son had gotten. Draper had then programmed his computerized flying program, Microsoft's Flight Simulator, to mimic the characteristics of the Boeing 737. He had spent over one hundred hours flying the 737 in his bedroom. All that would pay off huge dividends aboard Pacific Flight 571.

"Okay Dad, we need to level off."

Ross pushed the nose over slightly and reduced the power. It was flying fine with the gear still down. Normally, the gear would be raised on a missed approach. However, this was no normal operation. It was just an all-out "nuts and bolts" attempt to keep this aircraft in the sky.

"That's it. We're at two thousand feet. We need to turn right. I'll tell you when you're banking to much!"

Draper was still speaking through cupped hands into his father's left ear. He was confident that, with his father's abilities, and his own eyes and knowledge of flight, we could get this thing on the ground. Ross's pride in his son was almost enough to make him forget the pain in both eyes which prevented him from opening them. His own fifteen-year-old son had "stepped right up to the plate" and was saving the lives of passengers and crew. Ross's attention must stay on manipulating the controls, and must put his entire trust in Draper's instructions.

"That's thirty degrees of bank. Back off a little bit."

"Okay, you're heading is passing through two zero zero."

"Straighten out, you're heading two four zero. You're on downwind."

"Dad, how high do you want to climb?"

Ross held up four fingers.

"Okay, you're coming through three now, at about one thousand feet per minute. Your speed is one hundred and sixty knots."

Ross began a gentle push to arrest the rate of ascent. He also pulled the throttles back a little so that the speed wouldn't build up as he leveled off. There was no way the altitude and speeds were going to be perfect; "ballpark" was fine under the circumstances.

"Great, Dad. You're heading two four zero, at four thousand feet, speed one hundred and sixty knots."

Ross's blind flying took every bit of concentration he had, even to the exclusion of the pain in his eyes, filed with gritty dirt from the airport below. Now going straight and level, he signaled Draper, pointing to the autopilot.

"Do you want me to put on the autopilot?"

Ross nodded affirmatively.

Draper pressed the autopilot button and the aircraft was now flying on its own.

"What's he doing?" The General had asked.

"Maybe he's not going to land here," offered an aide.

"Well, he can't go too far. There can't be that much fuel left!"

"It looks like he's staying in the flight pattern."

Pacific Flight 571 continued on its downwind leg. Ross and Draper had to come up with a plan, and soon!

Ross turned his head around to the left. For the first time he had an opportunity to speak, or more accurately, yell, at the top of his voice.

"WATER!"

Draper only thought for a moment before realizing his Dad needed water to rinse his eyes out. Amidst the blasting air that was still entering the cockpit's right windshield, Draper unstrapped his seatbelt and went looking for water. He glanced at the instrument panel every few seconds, ready to run back and give information to his dad. The forward galley was a mess. Everything that hadn't been sucked out the window was strewn all over the floor. There in the midst of the pile was a coffeepot, the previous black liquid contents of which had splattered all over the walls.

Draper grabbed the pot and looked back to check on the flying. Ross was managing, with the autopilot engaged, to stay close to the heading, altitude, and airspeed. He stepped into the lavatory and filled the pot with water. He raced back to the jumpseat behind Ross, strapped in, and tapped him on the shoulder. Ross laid his head back as far as he could while keeping his left hand on the yoke, and his right hand on the throttles. Draper began to pour the water over his dad's eyes.

Ross forced himself to blink his eyes so the water could begin to rinse out the dirt. It was working. Small streams of brown gritty dirt began to parade down Ross's cheeks. Water was pouring all over the cockpit but was staying away from the instruments. When the pot was empty, Draper ran to fill it up again. As he poured, still more grime came out of the eyes. Ross was now able to keep his eyes open through the rinse. After three pots of water, Ross could keep his eyes open. Some blurring remained due to the scratches, but Ross could see well enough to fly the airplane. He turned around again, yelling with his right hand now helping to direct the words.

"I'm fine now! Great job, Son!"

Draper sat back in his seat, glowing at the pride coming from his dad. It wasn't so much the words. It was the look on Ross's eyes, as he turned around to deliver the words, which communicated much more.

Captain Ross Powers turned the aircraft back towards the airport. Once again, he verified the correct frequency for the ILS Approach to runway 6-Right. Even though it was visual conditions, Ross wanted the backup of his navigational equipment tracking the horizontal and vertical guidance to touchdown. As he neared the runway he made sure that no dirt was flying around that could cause the eye problem again.

Crossing the runway threshold again he began to flare. The touchdown was one of those "grease-jobs" that normally invoke applause from the passengers. There would be no applause today aboard Pacific Flight 571. Ross brought the airplane to a stop. The pure relief from the cessation of the roar of air was wonderful. For just a few moments Ross allowed his hearing to adjust. Then, he began to taxi the aircraft toward the gate area, wondering about what would surely be the wrath of the whole world against him.

As the aircraft was taxied into the gate, and after the ground crewman signaled that the ground electrics were plugged in, Ross pulled the fire handles of both engines. This was the only way they could be shut down since the fuel levers had broken off during the earlier struggle. Pulling the fire handle shuts off all liquids to an engine during an emergency engine fire procedure. This was now a convenient way for Ross to shut off the fuel to the engine, thereby causing it to quit.

No one was opening the forward exit door from the outside, as is usually the case. The jetway had not been pulled up by the side of the aircraft. In fact, there was no jetway operator in sight.

A booming loudspeaker from somewhere near the airplane rang out.

"Attention! Attention!" It got everyone's ear.

"Mobile stairs are pulling up to the aft entry door."

The authoritative voice continued, "All passengers are to depart from the rear entry door."

Then, more instructions, "All passengers are to exit first, followed by the crew."

The idea was to get the passengers out of the way in the event gunfire erupted.

Ross, and those near him, could sense the anticipation of trouble. Erica, Janie, the Marshall, and Pastor John all decided to wait and exit the aircraft with the captain. They had intuitively reasoned that their presence would prevent a possible catastrophe.

Special stairs were pulled up to the rear of the aircraft and the passengers exited out a rear entry door. Harold and Michael left with the passengers. Even though they are part of the crew they decided to rush out anyway. As they did, they both began yelling.

"He's got a gun! He's got a gun!"

That caused tension to mount even higher than it already was.

The bullhorn rang out again, "Captain Powers, exit the aircraft from the rear exit with your hands in the air!"

Draper joined his father. Together they made their way to the rear exit followed by Erica, close behind, being helped by Janie, Frank, and Pastor Chuck. As Ross and Draper began to descend down the stairs, a loud "pop" of the single shot could be heard, which echoed across the airport and sounded like six or seven shots in a row, each fading in volume from the one preceding it.

"Hold your fire! Hold your fire!" the voice on the loudspeaker was shouting.

There were no more shots. Everyone, military and civilian alike, struggled to regain their calm. Everyone realized what tragic pandemonium would occur if panic took over. One shot was bad enough. Hopefully, there would be no need for more gunfire.

Ross had hesitated near the top of the stairway and pushed Draper back in towards the aircraft as the shot rang out. He noticed that Erica had been standing behind him the whole time. Ross began the descent down the stairway alone, with his hands raised.

As he reached the bottom of the stairs he was immediately thrown face down to the pavement and handcuffed. Draper, now racing past Erica and down the stairway was yelling.

"Let him go, please, let my dad go!"

As the others made their way down the stairs most of the attention had already been diverted to the activity surrounding Ross's arrest. The news cameras were aimed toward Ross until someone mentioned that the pregnant woman, the one whose abortion was prohibited by the overzealous lunatic pilot, was coming down the stairs.

"There she is," someone shouted.

He hadn't intended to shoot. There was just this force, that seemed to come from somewhere outside his own realization, that applied just enough pressure to the trigger. Fortunately, the airman's intentionally high aim was sending the bullet to somewhere above and beyond the aircraft, where it would do no damage. It had left the M16's barrel going about 2000 miles per hour, or over 29,000 feet per second, and would travel that 70 feet in a about 1/500th of a second. However, at the last 1/2000th of a second, it seemed like an evil and invisible hand reached into time and space to deflect the deadly projectile to a new target, one that shocked the shooter himself.

The buzz of activity now shifted to Erica as she made her way slowly and seemingly painfully down the stairway. When she reached the tarmac she fainted. As she fell, her coat swung open from the front revealing a half-dollar size blood spot on her abdomen.

Erica hadn't realized herself that the errant bullet fired moments earlier had entered her abdomen just above the navel. It hadn't produced pain when it hit. Now as she lay on the tarmac medical personnel were scrambling to get the nearby standing ambulance to the side of the airplane.

Dr. Bell saw his opportunity. "She is going into labor. Get her to Anchorage General, now!" The hospital was only 10 minutes away. Dr. Bell figured he had plenty of time. He was wrong.

"She's been shot," shouted the first ambulance EMT that examined her as she was placed into the ambulance. He also recognized the obvious.

"The baby's coming, now," he shouted.

Janie, who had now exited the aircraft, ran to help.

Within moments the child was delivered. However, instead of a pink squirrelly baby boy, the EMT held in his hands the remains of a dead child, bleeding from the fatal bullet wound to the head.

Everything came to a stop. Everyone held still, it seemed. Activity appeared to be frozen in time for a few moments. Even the guards escorting Captain Powers stopped to see what had happened. All eyes were focused on the ambulance.

Everyone heard the EMT cry out.

"The baby is dead! He was shot in the head while still in his mother's womb."

Janie began to sob. It was the only sound that could be heard. Then after another minute, silence again.

The first sound to break that silence was the ringing of Dr. Bell's satellite phone. He had been standing there in some sort of shock. After several rings he pressed the "send" button and placed the phone up to his ear.

"Dr. Bell, Dr. Bell, can you hear me?"

Bell did not respond. He just stood there.

"Dr. Bell, this is the President," the unanswered voice went on.

"Ron Tallmadge and I are both on the phone. What is going on? Dr. Bell? Dr. Bell?"

David Bell couldn't speak. The gunshot wound in the baby's head had been a shock, even to him. For several moments he stood there, frozen. The sight of the wound caused his mind to flash back to his own gunshot wound, that night in Sacramento. In split seconds, as if on fast-forward, he began to retrace the events from the bathroom at Burger Barn, through the recovery, the impact on his life and family, all of it.

His eyes began to blur as he suddenly realized what a terrible turn his life had taken in the last several years. It was as if something, some power, some force of evil, released him at that moment. In an instant he had some clarity of thought that allowed him to see, in his mind, the faces of his wife and children he had once loved so much. He began to feel sadness, and then suddenly became overcome with grief, an emotion, like all the rest, that had been non-existent in his life for the last seven years.

The contingent of NOF representatives who, at the direction of the President, had been the only non-military people allowed on the airport, began a celebration.

In unison, with voices raised, they began to shout: "Pro Choice! Pro Choice! Pro Choice..."

No one saw, or could have ever predicted, the next event as Dr. David Bell methodically set his brown leather briefcase to the tarmac. He calmly dialed in the correct combination and opened it, removing 38-caliber pistol, which he had retrieved earlier from Graves. With the satellite phone in one hand, David used his remaining hand to place the muzzle of the 38 to his temple.

It was a deafening sound that caused everyone to drop to the ground. Then a uniformed figure began to move toward Dr. Bell's body. It was General Keith Dryer. Attention drew to the lifeless doctor, and briefly to the sickening sight of the mass of bloody brain tissue near the body.

Everyone thought the General was going to the doctor's aid.

However, Dryer didn't bother even taking a pulse. Instead, he concentrated on prying an object out of the tightly gripped hands of the dead doctor.

Then everyone thought the General was going after the gun.

However, it soon became obvious that the object of the General's now frantic attempt to pry open from the locked fingers was the satellite phone. It finally came loose.

He pressed it to his ear. "Yes Sir, Mr. President, this is General Dryer." "I have the situation completely in control."

After listening again for three seconds, "Yes Sir, The fetus was, uh, aborted." He listened for a few more seconds.

"Yes Sir. They are being taken into custody."

All eyes were now on the General as he listened to the President.

The General spoke again. "Yes, thank you, Mr. President, I'll look forward to that as well."

The smile on the General's face was enough of a cue to many in the crowd, who began shouting again, "...Pro Choice! Pro Choice! Pro Choice...," oblivious to the fact that their beloved leader, Paula Graves, lies somewhere over southeast ranges of Alaska, buried beneath the frozen snow upon which her body landed.

Further south, 30 mile from the Anchorage area, a blue and white 747 began a slow 180 degree turn. There would be no need to land at Anchorage today. The number one passenger should stay clear of the events that just occurred and Anchorage International Airport. For now, Air Force One was headed back to Washington DC. There would be a secret fuel stop along the way.

Air Force II, carrying the press, would follow.

Ross and Frank Grafton were ushered at gunpoint into awaiting armored military vehicles.

As they were driven away Ross looked back through a small plate window to see Draper standing…staring…helpless…yet managing to form the words on his lips to communicate, "I love you, Dad."

"Where are we being taken, Lieutenant?" Frank asked.

"To the brig at Elmendorf," came the reply. "From there you will most likely be sent to a Federal Prison while awaiting trial."

"Trial!" Now, Ross spoke up. "Do you have any idea on what charges?"

The answer would not come until morning. In the meantime Ross and Frank occupied separate cells at the Elmendorf Air Force Brig.

Mary Powers had followed the news all day. She knew that the portrayals of her husband were totally false as they were broadcast on national news.

"Mom, they've arrested Dad." Draper phoned home just after being allowed in the terminal.

Mary had called upon all her strength to sound encouraging to her young son. As she hung up the receiver after the short call she buried her face in her hands and began to weep. After several minutes, she went to her knees in prayer.

Captain Ross Powers sat in his lonely cell. It was a strange sight… a fully uniformed airline captain seated on a steel bench behind the cold steel bars of the cell. As Ross pondered the events of the day he struggled to mentally visualize specific particulars of the entire day, but failed as it all rolled into a hazy blur. He had never been incarcerated before. There was a mixture of confusion and apprehension, having no idea, or control, over the circumstances. This was alien to an airline captain who felt he was equipped to handle most everything that life dealt out.

From the blur that results from the brain trying to sort out dozens of thoughts into one at a time came bits and pieces of words and phrases that Ross had read in the bible at various times in his past.

"Trust in the Lord with all your heart...They that trust in the Lord...renew strength...wings of eagles...seek first...not given the spirit of fear..."

Ross yielded to these mental phrases. He began to reason that the only solidity he could benefit by in this totally complex atmosphere was the truths of the bible.

"What could I concentrate on?" Ross asked himself.

Immediately, without any conscious attempt, the 23rd Psalm came to his head. He wondered first if he could still remember the words

"The Lord is my Shepherd, I shall not want."

"Okay, Lord, I'm going to go for it here. I want you to be my shepherd. I want to trust in you." He continued, "I am separated from my family, I'm in jail, and all because I did what I think was right. You have got to be in this thing. Help me, God!"

Ross began to think of the next line.

"You make me to lie down in green pastures."

In the next cell sat Frank Grafton, also arrested and charged with a myriad of serious Federal crimes. Frank could barely hear Ross praying. It was just enough of a sound, barely above a whisper, that caught his ear.

"Captain Powers," Frank called in a hushed voice. "What are you doing?"

There was no answer.

"Ross!" Frank was less formal now. "How are you? What are you doing?"

Ross looked up. "Frank, I'm praying. Would you like to join me?"

"Yes, Ross, but as you know, I'm a little new to this."

And there in those dismal cells two men of God...on cold cement floors...hands joined through black rusted bars...kneeling...praying...

Later, at peace, both men slept. They would not wake until the bright morning sun poured in through the barred windows.

The fog had lifted from San Francisco by the next morning. Mary had bought a ticket to Anchorage on the first flight out. She would have normally used one of the free passes that airline employees and families have the benefit of. However, due to the previous day's fog cancellations Mary didn't want to chance getting "bumped" and decided to purchase a "positive space" ticket.

The airport terminal was still congested as many passengers who had been stuck in San Francisco for two days clamored to find flights out to various destinations. There seemed to be no awareness of the happenings surrounding the previous day's Pacific Flight 571.

However, Mary did notice a few stares from other crew members who recognized her as the wife of Captain Ross Powers.

She dismissed it as being imagined. She elected to not allow herself to be distracted from an attitude of prayer. After all, her husband was incarcerated and her son was alone in Anchorage, Alaska. She had been relieved to have learned last night that Draper had checked himself into a hotel, something most fifteen year olds would have difficulty doing. However, Draper was, of course, known to be "resourceful."

To Mary, the flight to Anchorage seemed much longer than the normal five and a half hours. She sat in a middle seat in coach about three rows from the last. On each side of her sat overweight men who squeezed Mary to the point of being uncomfortable. However, she continued to pray silently, eyes closed for most of the flight. One of the men attempted to make flirtatious conversation with this very attractive woman, only to notice her lips slightly moving in prayer. He wisely decided to leave her alone.

Even though it took Mary almost twenty-five minutes to get off the plane once it parked at the gate she bolted from the gate area in a dead run. She was going to check on Draper first, then find out where her husband was jailed. Dialing Draper's hotel number from her cell phone she concurrently hailed a taxi from the door just outside of the arrival section. She instructed the driver to go the Airport Hotel and then to wait while she took her bags in and got her son.

Draper was waiting in the lobby. He ran to his mother's arms and they embraced without a word. They both instinctively knew that there was much to do that day. It included finding Ross and bringing the world down on whoever was responsible for his incarceration.

It took less than an hour to determine Ross's whereabouts. A few questions at the airport police office were met with enthusiastic answers. The airport police were still offended at being kept out of the previous day's events. They would help in any way they could and explained to Mary that Ross had been taken to the Elmendorf Air Force Base Brig.

The taxi ride to the base was twenty-five minutes. It was noon when they arrived. They were stopped at the entrance gate by the normal contingent of Air Force Police, "APs." The base had been put on somewhat of a lock-down due to the unusual activation of emergency procedures the day before. Mary was insistent on being taken to the brig. However, the only location they would be allowed to go would be to the Air Force Legal Unit. Mary and Draper were required to exit the taxi and be escorted to the Legal Unit by APs.

Mary and Draper were met at the Legal Unit by a young airman who led them into a waiting room. After only a ten minute wait they were ushered into the office of the on-duty legal officer, First Lieutenant Joshua Casey. He was not in his office yet but was expected within a few minutes. The young airmen politely asked if they would like a cup of coffee or a coke. Both declined but were taken aback slightly by the kindness of the young man.

While sitting there in the office Mary began to sense an amazing peace. It was if the Lord had led them to this very place. When she looked at Draper she noticed him smiling while looking at the desk. There, in six inch wooden letters, where the initials "JC." This became one of several little hints that they were in the right place. On the credenza behind the desk was a small metal cross. There was also a plaque on the wall that contained the words from John 14:6,

"Jesus said unto him, I am the way, the truth, and
the life: no man cometh unto the Father, but by me".

Mary and Draper then knew beyond doubt that they were smack dab in the center of God's will. When Lieutenant Joshua Casey walked into the office they were even more convinced. His gracious and loving demeanor were evident at first look. Mary and Draper were speechless. Joshua walked right over to where they were sitting, knelt down, and said, "I will do everything possible to free your courageous husband as soon as possible. And, with the Lord's help, it might even happen today".

Tears flooded Mary's eyes as all the tension of the last twenty-four hours vanished in sweet release. Joshua explained how he had been at the Commander's office and had argued vehemently that the Air Force had no justification for imprisoning the men. Since Major General Keith Dryer was already on his way aboard an Air Force transport to Washington D.C., the base was, therefore, under the command of the Vice Commander, who coincidentally had objected to the use of Air Force personnel in yesterday's event.

The phone rang in the room next to Lieutenant Joshua Casey's office. The young airman stepped in and said that there was an important call for the Lieutenant, who elected to step out of his office to take the call. Mary and Draper sat hoping that it would be good news but, after twenty minutes of waiting had given up some hope.

Suddenly they heard some commotion from the adjoining room. Then, there he was... Ross Powers walked through the door and into the waiting arms of his wife and son. There was shock and relief all rolled up into one. For several minutes no words were spoken as this family was reunited after very traumatic events. Joshua Casey simply stood aside and smiled. After a few minutes Ross stepped back and motioned for someone else standing and waiting in the next room.

"Frank Grafton, I'd like you to meet my wife and son."

Back in San Francisco the publicity surrounding the events of Pacific Flight 571 was just starting to heat up. The organizers of the Anchorage Pro-Life rally had been making calls to friends, relatives, and church members regarding yesterday's events. The information spread among the San Francisco area churches like a wildfire.

The brunt of this growing public furor was being directed at Pacific Airlines, and reservation cancellations were coming in by late afternoon. The airline stood to lose millions of dollars of revenue due to the stand for abortion it appeared to take.

An emergency meeting of the Pacific Airlines Board of Directors was called for that evening. There were enough Christians on the board to call for the immediate resignations of the airline president and the chief pilot. A press conference was called for the next morning during which the board chairman announced those resignations and declared that Captain Ross Powers would be immediately reinstated.

Captain Ross Powers, Mary, Draper, and Frank Grafton had all been aboard a late flight the same evening of the board meeting. An emergency call from the chairman of the board to the Anchorage ticket counter resulted in VIP treatment for the four passengers. They were moved to First Class. The First Class passengers had been moved to coach and given two free round trips each for the inconvenience.

As a complete surprise, the First Class flight attendant was Janie Stone. It had been offered her to simply ride as a passenger that day. However, when she heard who the passengers were going to be she insisted on being the First Class attendant. Thirty-some hours after the tragic events of Pacific Flight 571, most of the participants were joined together in a joyous reunion aboard Pacific Flight 175. No-one noticed the irony of the inverted flight numbers.

Ross received a conference phone call within one hour of arriving home. On the phone was the newly appointed president of the airline and the new chief pilot. Ross was advised that he could return to flying at the time of his choice. He could also choose to stay in flight test or to simply return as a line Captain.

"I'd like to return to the line, if that's all right. And, if possible, I'd like a few days off to relax and then begin flying again at the first of the following month," which was only seven days in the future.

Returning to the line Ross found reactions to him in two differing types. Most of his fellow pilots would smile and pat him on the back. Others would sneer and even ignore him. Ross could clearly distinguish those that approved of his actions from those who did not. This didn't bother him as he actually felt sorry for the ones that seemed to reject anyone who might be considered a Christian.

Having witnessed what could only be described as miracles, Ross's new commitment to serving the Lord provided a change to his previous priorities. While still insistent on being the best pilot he could be he saw it more of a calling from God rather than some obsession with one's profession.

Chapter 11   San Diego

In the city of San Diego, California, a locally owned television station had decided, many years ago, to form a network of family oriented programming. It caught on so well that the United Broadcasting Company now owned stations throughout the world.

Slowly, due to the conversion to Christianity of the founder of United Broadcasting a few years earlier some of the programs were being replaced by popular bible teachers. Within two years all of the programming had changed, and the United Broadcasting Company was now being known as a Christian network.

The growth was phenomenal and required the world wide travelling of company officers and personnel as new stations were coming on board around the world. When the owners began to research the necessity of acquiring an aircraft someone mentioned a story they had heard about an airline captain who had taken a courageous stand against abortion.

The phone rang in Ross Powers' home.

"Captain Powers, my name is Brent Wood and I'm the President of United Broadcasting."

He continued, "Would you consider meeting with us to discuss our aviation needs?"

Immediately, Ross had a peace about this call and agreed to fly to San Diego that afternoon to meet with them. It hadn't been mentioned to him but they had already decided to purchase a business jet and planned to offer Ross the opportunity to run the flight department.

At the meeting there was no time wasted in getting right to the point.

"Ross, we have just placed an order for a Gulfstream 650 and would like you to fly it for us."

Ross thought for just a minute. No-one knew that Ross had been praying for an opportunity to be more active in serving the Lord. Additionally, he had reached the point with Pacific Airlines where he could retire with full retirement benefits. It seemed almost too good to be true.

"Gentlemen, I'm honored that you would consider me for this. I'd like to discuss this with my family and get back to you in a few days."

Ross didn't reveal to them how excited he was about the opportunity and was anxious to call Mary as soon as he got to his rental car. Unbeknownst to Ross, Mary had been praying since the Anchorage incident that Ross would be given an opportunity to be in the ministry.

"Honey, they offered me the position of Chief Pilot."

"Oh Ross, that is an answer to prayer. What did you tell them?"

"I told them that I'd get back to them soon. What do you think I should do?" He asked, while silently praying for the right answer.

"Ross, it is completely up to you and the Lord. I will support any decision you make."

"Thanks, Babe. I'm going to take it. I'm going to let them know right away."

And with that Ross made the next exit and got back on the highway in the direction of United Broadcasting Company. He knocked on the front door only to see the board members get up from their knees.

"Gentlemen, I'm sorry for the intrusion. I'd like to accept your offer!"

The five board members looked smilingly at each other. One proclaimed, "That's the fastest answer to prayer I've ever seen!" Handshakes soon gave in to hugs as these men began a long and fruitful relationship together.

Epilogue

Ross Powers spent the next several years flying for United Broadcasting Company. When not flying he would appear as a guest on many Christian programs speaking of the events of Pacific Airlines Flight 571. A Christian book publisher approached him about writing a book.

Draper Powers completed high school and was accepted in the Air Force and Naval academies. He chose the Navy and upon graduating from the academy he was immediately accepted into naval flight training. He later enjoyed several years as a pilot for The Blue Angels. He later became a pilot with Pacific Airlines.

Janie Stone and her husband would ultimately have four children. She retired from her job as Pacific Airlines flight attendant one month after Pacific Flight 571.

Frank Grafton flew only five more flights as a US Air Marshall. He retired and lives in Silver Spring, Maryland. He also has opportunities to speak of his experiences on Christian TV. He and Ross get together often.

Erica Paige became the church secretary at Pastor Chuck's church in San Jose. She later married as assistant pastor and became a stay-at-home mom to four children.

Nathan Lambert won a Pulitzer prize for his book detailing the events of Pacific Flight 571. He later wrote the screen play and a popular movie was produced.

Pastor John Wright never retired. He pastors to this day

For additional copies, contact
flightsongbooks@gmail.com

Made in the USA
Charleston, SC
21 September 2010